CHOOL OF FEAR

BY GITTY DANESHVARI

School of Fear
Class is Not Dismissed!
The Final Exam

SCHOOL OF FEAR

CLASS IS **NOT** DISMISSED!

BY

GITTY DANESHVARI

ILLUSTRATED BY

CARRIE GIFFORD

www.atombooks.net/tween

ATOM

First published in the United States in 2009 by Little, Brown
Books for Young Readers
First published in Great Britain in 2012 by Atom

A CIP catalogue record for this book
is available from the British Library.

ISBN 978-1-907411-67-0

Printed and bound in Great Britain by
Clays Ltd, St Ives plc

Papers used by Atom are from well-managed forests
and other responsible sources.

MIX
Paper from
responsible sources
FSC® C104740

Atom
An imprint of
Little, Brown Book Group
100 Victoria Embankment
London EC4Y 0DY

An Hachette UK Company
www.hachette.co.uk

www.atombooks.net/tween

For Sophia Coco

SCHOOL OF FEAR

SCHOOL OF FEAR

The wilderness outside Farmington, Massachusetts
(Exact location withheld for security purposes)
Direct all correspondence to: PO Box 333, Farmington, MA 01201

Dear Contestants,

Much like homework, pimples, and puberty, your second summer at School of Fear is not optional. Any acts of insubordination such as claiming death of a beloved pet, amnesia, or enrollment in sleepaway camp will be met by my lawyer Munchauser—quite literally. The man with the dirtiest fingernails in all of America shall arrive at your home with dental floss in hand. Munchauser, who has only thrice been to a dentist, shall then proceed to floss his small yellow teeth mere inches from your face. This is an act from which you will not recover.

The summer course shall begin promptly at 9:00 AM on Saturday May 29th at the base of Summerstone. And do remember to guard School of Fear's anonymity by running the bath, blaring the television, and playing the harmonica whenever discussing our institution. On behalf of myself, my comb-over-clad assistant Schmidty, Macaroni the bulldog, and my highly trained cats, we look forward to seeing all of your Vaseline-coated smiles terribly soon.

Fondest regards,

Mrs. Wellington

MRS. WELLINGTON
Headmistress, School of Fear
49-Time Pageant Winner

P.S. Munchauser is not the slightest bit interested in seeing any of you again, and requested that I tell you all as much.

CHAPTER 1

EVERYONE'S AFRAID OF SOMETHING:

Heliophobia is the fear

of the sun.

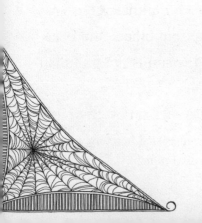

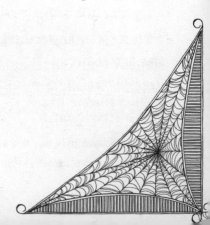

The sun is not the sun. And that isn't to say that the sun is the moon, for that is most definitely not the case. The sun is simply far more than the center of the solar system or a bright shiny thing in the sky. Day after day the sun wrestles us from darkness, bringing with it the many secrets we hide from others and occasionally even ourselves. Oh yes, the sun is the guardian of truth, whether we like it or not.

Thirteen-year-old Madeleine Masterson breezed into

Boston, utterly delighted to have escaped the dreary skies of London. With a beaming smile the fair-skinned, blue-eyed girl with raven locks just shy of her shoulders led her parents into the blazing heat and humidity. The entire Masterson family stood outside warming their chilly British bones in the extraordinary sunshine. For the English, the sun is a bit like the Queen; they know she exists but they simply don't see her that often.

Only a year earlier, Madeleine had been a shell of her current self, walking through life in abject terror, certain that enemies lurked around every corner, or rather *in* every corner. Mr. and Mrs. Masterson's only child had long suffered from a dreadful phobia of spiders and other insects. In addition to wearing a netted veil and a belt of repellents at all times, Madeleine had refused to enter any building that had not been fumigated recently by an exterminator. As one might imagine, most of her classmates' parents refused to meet the extensive and expensive guidelines necessary before Madeleine could enter their residences. Thus Madeleine missed out on slumber parties, birthdays, and all outdoor activities.

Most fortunately for all involved, Madeleine had spent the previous summer at the highly clandestine, word-of-mouth institution known as School of Fear. Much to her parents' delight, Madeleine had returned veil- and repellent-free, an absolutely changed child. Well, not entirely changed; the young girl remained fascinated by world leaders, often listing United Nations delegates in alphabetical order for entertainment. But long gone was her crippling arachnophobia.

"Mummy and Daddy, not to be impertinent, but why are you sending me back for another summer? I'm cured, fixed, or however you care to put it. Might I remind you that I am now a member of the Spider Appreciation Club as well as Eight-Legged Creatures for Social Change?"

"Yes, we know, dear. Your father and I are both terribly impressed with your progress," Mrs. Masterson said with a smile.

"Aren't you the only member of those clubs?" Mr. Masterson inquired.

"That is hardly the point, Daddy," Madeleine replied huffily.

"Unfortunately, as we've explained, it's a contractual issue. Mrs. Wellington's attorney, that ghastly man Munchauser, had us sign a two-summer agreement. He claims the second session is necessary to reinforce the progress you made last summer. But not to worry, dear. Next summer you will be free to do anything you like."

"Well, I suppose another summer won't hurt me too badly. Plus I am terribly keen to see the others again and have a proper catch-up," Madeleine acquiesced as the town car turned onto a narrow cobblestone road. Within seconds the car was shrouded in darkness cast by the trees and sticky vines that grew from one side of the road to the other, creating a tunnel. Although hard to decipher in the faint light, a multitude of homemade signs warned against entering the Lost Forest. The densely wooded area had quite the reputation for chewing people up and *not* spitting them out.

The car slowed as the foliage tunnel opened at the base of a large granite mountain. Mr. and Mrs. Masterson had planned to exit the vehicle and meet this Schmidty character they had heard so much about. However, the soaring temperatures quickly dissuaded the London natives from leaving the air-conditioned confines of their car. Sporting an orange tartan dress with a matching headband and a massive grin, Madeleine bounded out of the sedan. Technically speaking, it was more of a saunter than a bound, due to the blistering weather. Madeleine was beginning to understand what people meant by too much of a good thing.

Seated on lawn chairs under a large umbrella were Schmidty, School of Fear's trusty cook/groundskeeper/wig groomer, and Macaroni, the English bulldog.

"Schmidty!" Madeleine yelped joyfully, before stopping. The young girl was utterly gobsmacked and unable to speak. The plump old man was dressed in a Hawaiian shirt, polyester black shorts, and open-toed sandals that showcased his furry feet and jagged brown toenails. But most offensive was the sight of his fallen comb-over; a mess of gray ringlets was all that remained. Madeleine stared for a few seconds before regaining her composure and assessing how best to handle the delicate situation.

"Schmidty, I'm awfully sorry to inform you, but your hair—"

"Please, Miss Madeleine," Schmidty interrupted, "it's too painful to hear confirmation. I'm attempting a state of denial, but you know it's much harder than Mrs. Wellington makes it look."

Madeleine nodded in agreement before patting Schmidty on the shoulder. In light of the heat and the fallen comb-over, Madeleine thought it best to avoid a hug.

CHAPTER 2

EVERYONE'S AFRAID OF SOMETHING:

Syngenesophobia is the fear

of relatives.

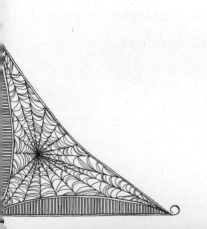

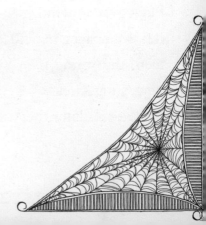

As Madeleine fanned both herself and Macaroni with a magazine, a bumper-sticker-covered VW bus screeched around the corner, smoke literally rising off the cobblestones. Through the condensation and bug-covered windshield Madeleine was able to make out a teenager behind the wheel. No more than nineteen, the young man was wearing a baseball cap and large sunglasses.

Seconds later the VW bus jerked to a standstill and

the back door swung open, releasing a wobbly Theodore Bartholomew. The chubby brown-haired boy with glasses was dressed in salmon golf shorts, a turquoise polo shirt, Top-Sider sailing shoes, and a plaid fanny pack. All in all, there was very little that was redeeming about his outfit.

"I'm telling Mom and Dad, Joaquin! *Do you hear me?* You promised them you wouldn't drive over forty miles an hour. And even with my life flashing before my eyes, I could see that the speedometer was at fifty," thirteen-year-old Theo shrieked at his older brother as he unloaded two bags.

Theo was a nervous New Yorker, a child who had grown up worrying that danger or even death was waiting for him and his family around every bend. The youngest of seven children, Theo had exhausted his family with his theatrical displays of concern, most notably his Dead or Alive tracking system. Prior to attending School of Fear, Theo had tracked his family relentlessly, logging their status dead or alive, in his trusty notebook. He had also spent vast quantities of time writing letters to the mayor of New York on ways to make the city safer. Much to Theo's annoyance, the mayor never responded—not even to his proposal for a citywide law requiring all residents to use antibacterial hand sanitizer on an hourly basis. Theo had seen the slogan as something catchy yet firm: "The mayor says use Purell or we'll lock you in a cell."

Under the blazing summer sun, Joaquin stared at his high-strung younger brother and sighed.

"Listen, grandpa," Joaquin mumbled in response to Theo's speeding accusation.

"Do not take our grandfather's name in vain. And for the last time, this is *sportswear casual,* not retirement chic. And I will have you know, it's very *in* this summer."

"Can't you ever just chill?" Joaquin remarked with obvious annoyance.

"Seriously, Theo, chill," Lulu Punchalower seconded as she exited the front seat of the van dressed in an old tee shirt, denim shorts, and a pair of black Converse sneakers. Thirteen-year-old Lulu's strawberry blond hair had grown longer and wavier in the year since she'd left School of Fear. However, the green eyes Lulu so often rolled back in her head still shone as bright as ever among her sea of freckles.

On the surface the Providence, Rhode Island, native had changed very little since coming to School of Fear. Lulu remained hardheaded, sarcastic, with more than a penchant for speaking her mind. However, if one looked closer, there were multiple small yet important shifts. Lulu was now able to enjoy water and other beverages throughout the day, forgoing her ban on liquids to avoid using restrooms without windows. Before School of Fear, Lulu had been a claustrophobic who would have done almost anything to avoid confined spaces, including handcuffing herself to cars, toilets, and even the odd stranger. Thankfully Lulu now left the job of carrying handcuffs to law-enforcement officers and a few over-zealous mall cops.

"Chill," Theo repeated back to Lulu. "Don't imitate Joaquin's speech. He is a derelict. A true degenerate. Did you know that he is currently in the process of repeating the twelfth grade? And they won't even let the juvenile delinquents hang out with him because they think *he's* a bad influence on *them*. He was voted most likely to shoplift from Rite Aid. That is *not* a good thing!" Theo bellowed as his glasses steamed over from the intense humidity.

"Theo, don't be jealous. Your brother's just naturally cooler than you are."

"See ya, Lu," Joaquin said before offering Lulu a fist bump and heading back to the car.

"*Lu?* You gave her a nickname? What about me? I am your own flesh and blood, and I have been asking for a nickname for years!"

"Later, Theo," Joaquin mumbled as he slammed the van door and started the engine.

"Don't embarrass our DNA; give me a hug goodbye," Theo shrieked as the van pulled away. "I should have been Italian; they appreciate family...and pasta."

"Lulu! Theo!" Madeleine exclaimed cheerfully as she ambled out from under the umbrella toward her friends.

"Now *this* is a proper reaction to seeing a friend," Theo said judgmentally to Lulu before embracing Madeleine.

"Will you relax? I'm not much of a hugger. Big deal," Lulu snapped back while offering her fist to Madeleine.

"I'm terribly sorry, Lulu, but what exactly do you expect me to do with that? Is it like rock, paper, scissors?"

"Guys, this is how *cool* people say hello. They bump fists. *Joaq* taught it to me; apparently *everyone* does it, even Obama."

"All right," Madeleine said cheerfully before bumping fists with Lulu. "I do enjoy learning how dignitaries greet people."

Theo cleared his throat loudly while shooting daggers at Lulu.

"What?" Lulu asked with a shrug of the shoulders.

"Not only did you not hug me…"

"I bumped fists with you. Same thing, Theo. Even Maddie knows that, and she's from *England*."

"There are a multitude of manners to greet someone, Theo. We shouldn't be critical of which one Lulu prefers," Madeleine said calmly. "In Japan people bow, and in France they kiss each other on the cheeks."

"She *punched* me!" Theo yelled with sweat dribbling off his eyebrows, down his glasses, and onto his red chipmunkesque cheeks.

"No! You *fell* on my fist, which makes it totally your fault," Lulu passionately explained.

"*Fell on your fist?* If this were a court of law, the judge would laugh in your face. Perhaps even spit in your eye," Theo said as he attempted to wipe his fore-head on his sleeve. "Does anyone have a handkerchief? I'm drowning here."

"Miss Lulu, Mister Theo, I'm terribly sorry to inter-rupt, but—"

"Oh, Schmidty," Theo whimpered sweetly as he wad-dled with open arms toward the old man. "I've missed you so. There were even days when I almost missed the Casu Frazigu, and please note I said *almost,* so don't put any of it in my food."

"Dear Mister Theo, I don't know what to say. I'm ter-ribly touched that you've thought of me, and Madame's fondness for maggot cheese, at all."

"*Schm,* you and I are like family, only we're not related," Theo said dramatically. "If there weren't a vari-ety of serious health risks, I'd prick my finger and make you my blood brother."

"Did you just call him *Schm?*" Lulu asked harshly.

"Oh, I'm sorry, do you and *Joaq* have a monopoly on nicknames?" Theo hit back.

"How I've missed the endless and pointless argu-ments of Miss Lulu and Mister Theo," Schmidty mut-tered to himself.

"Hey, Schmidty," Lulu said warmly while putting out her fist, which Schmidty willingly bumped.

To reinforce the fact that even Schmidty knew how to fist-bump, Lulu shot Theo an unmistakably victorious glare, which he pretended not to see. And when Theo purported not to see something, he shot his eyes dramatically from right to left, then from sky to ground. He had never been very adept at subtlety.

"Macaroni. Oh, Macaroni," Theo uttered joyfully as he dropped next to the panting dog. "You really are man's best friend—not that anyone would have ever mistaken Lulu for that."

Lulu looked at Schmidty and Madeleine with an exasperated expression. "I've been stuck with him for almost five hours," she said, "which is four hours and fifty-five minutes over my limit."

"Miss Lulu, I must inquire how and why the two of you wound up in the same car."

"That was Theo's idea. Plus my parents didn't really want to make the drive again. They said they'd rather play golf."

"That's the thanks I get for saving the planet," Theo

said before taking a long pause. *"Carpooling is not a crime; it's an environmentally good time."*

"He wrote that himself," Lulu deadpanned.

"I did," Theo said proudly. "I see *big* things for that slogan, B-I-G."

"Why do you feel the need to spell *big?* We all know how to spell *big,* Theo," Lulu said with cresting annoyance.

"The important thing is that you're both here. I've been so keen to see you and hear about your terms," Madeleine interjected in a rather obvious attempt to break the tension.

"I totally forgot how you use weird English words like *keen.*" Lulu smirked. "It's not a bad thing, I had just totally forgotten until now."

"Ah, the underhanded Lulu insult. Bet you've missed that," Theo said loudly to Madeleine.

Unsure how to defuse the situation, Madeleine decided it was best to smile. As the young girl grinned, a light creepy-crawly sensation tickled her left arm. Without thinking, Madeleine jumped while simultaneously slapping herself.

"Oh, sorry, I thought I felt something on my arm. Not a spider, of course. Not that it would have bothered me, because I'm rather fond of spiders now. I was only concerned that it was an aggressive hummingbird, but it turns out it was just a strand of hair; it's rather easy to confuse the two."

"Why are we still outside?" Theo moaned.

"It *is* awfully humid," Madeleine acquiesced unsteadily. "I recently learned that two types of North American beetles like to lay eggs when it's humid. Isn't that interesting?"

"I've already lost two pounds in water weight. I'm beginning to feel like a model on the runway, all skin and bones," Theo grunted, completely ignoring Madeleine's observation.

"Well, not to worry, Theo. You certainly don't look like a model," Lulu retorted quietly.

"I'll have you know I've done some modeling in my time," Theo said while puffing out his chest with false bravado.

Lulu buckled over with laughter for a good thirty seconds before she could even manage to speak. "That is *such* a lie! *You* ... as ... a ... model. Ha!"

"It's true!" Theo shot back defensively.

"Oh, really? Then please tell me who you modeled for."

"It was for an article in a children's magazine. I believe the title of the story was 'Bagel Boys: The True Tale of Children Addicted to Carbohydrates,'" Theo said softly, before Lulu erupted again in laughter. "It still counts as modeling!"

"Schmidty, please tell me that Garrison's returning for the summer," Madeleine pleaded while watching Theo and Lulu bicker.

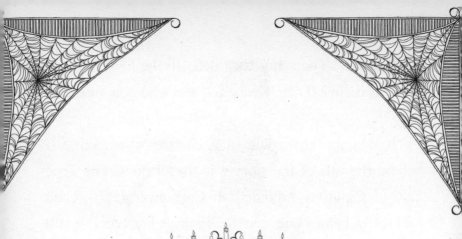

CHAPTER 3

EVERYONE'S AFRAID OF SOMETHING:

Erytophobia is the fear

of blushing.

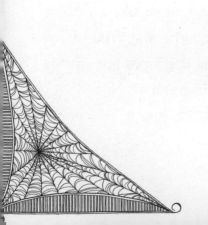
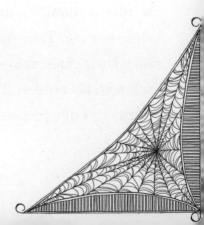

Madeleine, Lulu, Theo, Schmidty, and Macaroni all indulged in a grimace as they waited impatiently for fourteen-year-old Garrison Feldman's arrival. Although the boy was technically only ten minutes late, the robust humidity made it feel more like an hour. While waiting, Theo had squeezed his way onto Macaroni's lawn chair, mimicking the dog's position on his back with his arms and legs up in the air.

Just as Lulu prepared to launch into a critique of

Theo's inane behavior, a Jeep convertible pumping reggae music rounded the corner, with none other than Garrison Feldman in the front seat. Much as one would expect to see at the cinema, the sunlight perfectly silhouetted Garrison as he exited the car. He had grown taller and a great deal more tanned in the year since Lulu, Madeleine, and Theo had last seen him. His once neatly groomed blond locks now hung in a shaggy mess around his face.

Even dressed in surfer shorts, an old tee shirt, and flip-flops, there was simply no denying it: the boy was gorgeous. Fourteen-year-old Garrison grabbed his bag and boogie board, then cracked a magnetic smile at the group, instantly mesmerizing everyone. Even Theo was captivated by his striking appearance, or perhaps it was due to the fact that Garrison's glistening skin reminded him of a McDonald's French fry.

"What's up?" Garrison said warmly as he held out his hand for Schmidty to shake.

"Welcome back, Mister Garrison," Schmidty said with a smile.

Garrison returned the smile before extending his hand to Theo, who charged full force, engulfing him in a mammoth bear hug.

"My man, Gary! The boys are back together! Let the bro-mance continue!"

"Don't call me Gary," Garrison said as he pushed away a perspiring Theo. "And definitely don't use the word *bro-mance*. Ever. Not even when you're alone."

"Eww, you left a face print on his shirt," Lulu exclaimed, pointing to the sweat silhouette Theo had left behind.

Luckily, Garrison didn't notice, having already moved on to Madeleine, who was as red as beetroot, absolutely blushing with anticipation. While she hadn't admitted it to anyone, Madeleine often thought of Garrison fondly, especially on cold, gray London days. But now that he was standing in front of her, she was absolutely over-whelmed by the sensation of her crush.

"Maddie…"

"Hello, Garrison. Did you have a relaxing journey from Miami?" Madeleine asked nervously, speaking at an exceptionally fast speed.

Before he could answer, Madeleine gave him a quick hug and then averted her eyes in embarrassment. Lulu, sensing the awkwardness in the air, threw her left arm around Garrison's shoulders and playfully ruffled his hair.

"What's with the hair? It's almost longer than mine."

"I'm a surfer now," the formerly waterphobic boy announced proudly. "This is how the guys wear it."

"Um, isn't that a *boogie board?*"

"Why do you always have to point out people's short-comings, Lulu?" Theo harped. "And don't think I didn't notice you hugged him."

"Whatever."

"Dear misters and misses, as much as it pains me to break up this highly intellectual conversation, Madame is waiting, and you know how old she is. She really could die at any time . . ." Schmidty trailed off.

For the first time the students looked beyond Schmidty, to a large metal contraption at the base of the mountain. It looked somewhat like a grand metal bird-cage or, perhaps more morbidly, an ornate prison cell.

"What is that?" Lulu asked. "Not that I'm afraid, because I totally ride in elevators now, not that it's even an elevator. So, um, what exactly is that, Schmidty?"

"This is the latest addition to School of Fear: the Summerstone Vertical Tram," Schmidty explained while waking Macaroni from his heat-induced slumber.

"That is a pretty nice-looking *SVT*," Theo said in a knowledgeable manner.

"SV what?" Lulu asked with raised eyebrows.

"I made an executive decision—"

"But you're not an executive—"

"Fine, I made a *nonexecutive* decision to create an acronym. And let me tell you, acronyms are all the rage in NYC."

"Children, before you enter the SVT, as Mister Theo has coined it, Mac needs to perform a sniff-down for electronics, for, as you remember, Mrs. Wellington frowns upon cell phones, PDAs, BlackBerries, computers, and all other technological means of communication. And please don't think it's that I don't trust you. It's simply that Madame doesn't trust you. As of this morning she could barely remember if she liked you."

And with that, the drooling bulldog with large saggy eyes waddled up to the students' bags. Macaroni then sat down, his rear paws neatly positioned between his front paws, and began snorting. You see a bulldog simply cannot smell without snorting; it is an absolute impossibility. It's far more likely for a bulldog to speak English than to smell without snorting. In between vociferous sniffs, Macaroni also employed his tongue, licking not only the bags but the children's legs. And when he was all finished, Macaroni gave Schmidty a knowing glance before collapsing onto the cobblestones, utterly exhausted from exerting so much energy.

"I certainly don't mean to be cheeky, Theo, but I am flabbergasted that you didn't try to sneak in a mobile," Madeleine said honestly.

"What can I tell you, Maddie? You're looking at a changed *man*."

"Oh, brother," Lulu said with her traditional roll of the eyes. "He thinks he's a *man* now."

As Theo furrowed his brow with annoyance, Schmidty pulled a large key ring from the pocket of his black shorts and began searching for the correct key.

"Why even bother locking this? You worried about joyriders?" Garrison asked while tossing his blond hair out of his face.

"I was planning to let Madame explain, but as she rarely makes any sense, I suppose I ought to handle the situation," Schmidty said before clearing his throat. "Summerstone has been the target of a very persistent burglar over the past several months. I believe we are at robbery number seven, or is it eight? The number could actually be much higher, for we often can't tell things are missing for days," Schmidty said as he led the children and Macaroni onto the tram and closed the door.

"Have you spoken to the sheriff?" Madeleine inquired as the tram began to move up the mountain.

"We most definitely have spoken with the sheriff, but he's as perplexed as we are."

"Is it just me, or is this the slowest ride in the history of rides?" Lulu asked with a tense smile as the tram continued to rattle and bump up the mountain.

"So there haven't been any other burglaries in town, Schmidty?" Madeleine pressed on.

"Well, not really…"

"What does *not really* mean?"

"Well, there was a break-in at the Mancini Bakery, but all the burglar took were cupcakes, so the sheriff is pretty sure that young Jimmy Fernwood is behind it. His mother's had him on a rather strict no-sugar diet—"

"Always blaming the fat kids," Theo said critically. "Talk about racial profiling."

"Theo, I regret to inform you, but fat children do not constitute a race," Madeleine explained.

"Man, it's really getting stuffy in here. It's hard to breathe," Lulu said with a stressed expression.

"Lulu, we're in fresh air," Garrison responded.

"Does anyone else hear that chirping sound?" Madeleine asked with an anxious tone. "Out of curiosity, how far away do you think *they* are? You don't suppose they're on the tram with us?"

"Does this thing have an emergency phone or radio or flare gun, Schmidty?" Lulu interrupted just as the old man prepared to answer Madeleine's question.

"I'm afraid not, Miss Lulu. You know Madame, no dubious technologies."

"I feel like I need to stand up," Lulu said as a familiar pounding behind her left eye commenced. For as long as Lulu could remember, fear always manifested itself as a harsh pounding sensation behind her left eye.

"But you *are* standing up, Lulu," Madeleine explained sweetly.

"Um," Lulu said as her face scrunched up, "are we almost there? I feel like we've been in here for hours."

"Just about, Miss Lulu," Schmidty said as the SVT jolted to a stop at the top of the mountain.

Lulu pushed her way off the SVT first, then hunched

over with her hands on her knees and caught her breath.

"You know I'm not the litigious type, Schmidty, but this is a whiplash lawsuit waiting to happen. I'm a little surprised Munchauser let you put this in," Theo said as he followed the old man off the SVT.

"Ugh, Munchauser. Simply saying his name leaves a sour taste in my mouth," Schmidty said with the expression of a cat coughing up a hairball.

Garrison, the last to exit the SVT, had just placed his right foot on solid ground when the tram dropped two hundred feet to the base of the mountain. The metal bars slammed into the ground, setting off a thunderous series of sounds.

"Holy cannoli!" Theo shrieked as he dropped to his knees and covered his head with his hands. "The burglar is trying to kill us! There's a hit out!"

"How I loathe disappointing you, Mister Theo, but no one is trying to kill you."

"Yet," Lulu chimed in.

"I merely forgot to pull the brake on the SVT. I tend to do that rather frequently."

"Schmidty, I could have fallen two hundred feet and

crashed into the ground! Do you have any idea what an accident like that could do to an athlete's body? I didn't think it was possible, but this is worse than the wooden crane you dragged us up in last year," Garrison said angrily. "I mean, sure, the wood was cracked and held together by rubber bands and glue, but at least it didn't drop people!"

"I feel a tension headache coming on," Theo said as he massaged his temples. "We haven't even seen Wellington yet, and already I can't breathe, and my head is splitting."

"Um, in case you forgot, Theo, it was Garrison who almost plummeted two hundred feet, not you," Lulu said pointedly.

"Always getting caught up with the details," Theo said as he approached Summerstone's grand wrought-iron gate. The rusted old metal entry connected to a soaring slate wall that enclosed the four-acre island in the sky.

The foursome followed Schmidty and Macaroni through Summerstone's gate, where they met a very strange sight. The spotty green lawn was covered in tuxedo-clad scarecrows, BEWARE OF BEAUTY QUEEN signs, and seemingly endless booby traps. Thickly woven ropes crisscrossed the lawn both vertically and horizontally, linking cans to ladders to buckets to nets to odd-shaped metal objects to small glass jars to cages to bells, and so much more.

"Schmidty, you know I enjoy being crafty as much as the next guy—every Christmas I make my own ornaments with a little paste and glitter. But I got to tell you, when it comes to home security, you need a professional, none of this do-it-yourself baloney."

The old man simply stared in bemusement at Theo. The answer hardly needed to be said: this was security, Wellington-style.

CHAPTER 4

EVERYONE'S AFRAID OF SOMETHING:

Scelerophobia is the fear

of burglars.

Summerstone's foyer was grander in scale than that of the average mansion, but then again, this most certainly was not an average mansion. The pink fleur-de-lis wallpaper bubbled and buckled, proof of its many years in place. Freshly cut pale pink hydrangeas sat atop the round entry table, to the left of which an entire wall was dedicated to Mrs. Wellington's framed pageant photos.

The children placed their luggage at the base of the

staircase, next to which Macaroni performed a belly flop, his legs splayed out beneath him.

"It appears Macaroni has overexerted himself with all the napping, waddling, and snorting he's done this morning," Schmidty said.

As Macaroni peacefully snored, Schmidty guided the foursome to the Great Hall. Over the course of the year, each of the students had thought of the Great Hall and wondered if their memories were in fact accurate or if their recollections had grown more fantastical and whimsical than the reality. Theo had tried to explain the far-fetched design of the space to his parents, but as he had quite the reputation for exaggeration, neither his mother nor his father took the description very seriously. In fairness to the Bartholomews, the Great Hall certainly did not sound terribly real. After all, how often does one come across a majestic hall with a seemingly endless array of one-of-a-kind doors decorating nearly every inch, from the floor to the walls to the ceiling? Doors shaped like keyholes and pocket watches stood next to barn gates and the sides of airplanes. Some doors were so small only a mouse could use them, while others loomed so large an entire bus could pass throug the frame. And far off, at the very end of the lengthy corridor, was a floor-to-ceiling stained-glass portrait of Mrs. Wellington in her beauty-queen glory days, crown and all.

While none of them could have imagined it, the hall was truly more spectacular and bizarre than they had remembered. It took a certain level of absurdity and lunacy to create such a manor. This was a house that only Mrs. Wellington could have built.

Schmidty led the children to double white-and-gold doors, which he forcefully flung open, bringing both the sitting room and the classroom into view.

"May I present your honorable, fashionable, and highly youthful-looking teacher, Mrs. Wellington," Schmidty droned as if reading from a script.

Mrs. Wellington turned toward the children with an utterly blank expression. Not that they even noticed: they were far too distracted by the sight of her heavily made-up face. The old woman positively did not sub- scribe to the less-is-more motto where makeup was concerned. Clad in a sleeveless lavender dress with a

a gray scarf, Mrs. Wellington sashayed
ne foursome with a restrained smile. She ran
ds over her slightly disheveled brown bob wig
before stopping next to Schmidty.

"Who are these small people?"

"Your students, Madame. Perhaps you would care to greet them?"

"Do you mean to say my *contestants?*" Mrs. Wellington asked distrustfully.

"Yes, Madame, these are your returning contestants: Miss Lulu, Mister Theo, Mister Garrison, and Miss Madeleine."

"No, you are mistaken, my elderly one, these are not my contestants."

"And let the weirdness begin," Lulu mumbled to herself.

"Chubby is at least one and a half inches shorter and definitely a bit lighter, and Sporty's hair was neat and not nearly so blond, and as for Lulu..."

"Madame, must we go through this again?" Schmidty said with a sigh of exasperation. "Contestants grow every year, just like your hair used to."

"Those really were the days: haircuts, shampoo, con-

ditioner. Why, I'm getting teary-eyed, remembering."
Mrs. Wellington paused to dab her eyes with a lavender
handkerchief. "Now then, are we sure these so-called
contestants aren't imposters? You know how I feel about
imposters. I don't care for imposter crabmeat, let alone
people."

"Of course, Madame, but I assure you that these are
your contestants."

"Perhaps we should lock them in the gardener's shed
and send for their dental records, to be on the safe
side?"

"Madame, I think such an idea would be frowned
upon by their parents and perhaps even the sheriff."

"Yes, but what about identity theft? You mustn't forget what happened to me."

"Forgetting who you are hardly counts as identity
theft."

"Very well," Mrs. Wellington said while caressing the
soft gray fur around her neck. "Cashmere certainly isn't
what it used to be; this scarf smells of giblets."

"That's because it's a cat, Madame."

And indeed, it was a cat. Mrs. Wellington had a lean
gray cat wrapped stylishly around her neck.

"Don't be ridiculous," Mrs. Wellington said before pausing to look down. "Although it does appear to have a mouth. Oh, never mind! *You say tomahto, I say tomato; you say cat, I say scarf,*" Mrs. Wellington sang off-key.

"Now then, contestants, take your seats," Mrs. Wellington announced as she removed Fiona the cat from her neck and placed her on the floor.

Madeleine, Lulu, Theo, and Garrison took their seats in the manor's unusual classroom. The students' silver-leaf desks, arranged two per row, descended in size from normal to minuscule. At the head of the classroom, Mrs. Wellington leaned against her large gold-plated desk and nodded her head a few times. Madeleine stared, utterly mystified as to why the old woman was nodding. After all, no one had said anything for minutes. Not wishing to be impertinent, Madeleine smiled and nodded her head in return.

"What is this? Are you two signaling each other?" Theo asked Madeleine dramatically.

"Oh, dear, Theo. I was merely trying to be polite, as Mrs. Wellington was nodding."

"OK," Lulu jumped in. "Mrs. Wellington, who were you nodding at?"

"Yeah," Garrison grunted as Lulu finished. "Actually, I don't really care."

"Of all the invasions of privacy! The lot of you ought to be ashamed of yourselves," Mrs. Wellington said huffily. "I was nodding to *myself*. Honestly, can't a woman have a personal conversation with herself without you misfits eavesdropping?"

"Well, I can't speak for the others, but I didn't hear anything," Theo said sincerely.

Mrs. Wellington sighed and nodded her head at Theo.

"Was that for me, or are you having another conversation with yourself?" Theo spat out. "Am I the only one who finds this confusing?"

"We haven't time for your confusion, Theo; we are in the midst of a security breach. We've got a code magenta with a splash of teal, and you know how serious *that* is."

"I don't," Theo quickly answered.

"Not to be cheeky, Mrs. Wellington, as I'm not American, but I believe Homeland Security's color advisory system goes from green to red without stopping at magenta or teal."

"Homeland what? Is that some sort of hippie commune? I am talking about the Pageant Colors of Crime. Have you learned nothing at school? Everyone knows magenta is burglaries and teal is odd behavior from a mysterious man."

"I can't believe you brought us back here in the middle of a crime wave. Thanks a lot, lady," Theo said while ruefully shaking his head. "I might as well have taken an internship on Riker's Island!"

"Yeah, not to mention the fact that if you hadn't dragged us back here, I could be playing Wii right now," Lulu added.

"How dare you? I brought you back here because you *need* me! You are far from cured of your phobias. The fact that I have been unable to find a security team willing to aid in the burglary investigation in exchange for signed pageant photos of myself was of no consequence in my decision."

"Mrs. Wellington, we get it. You missed us. We're touched, but we're cured," Theo said gently.

"Is that so?"

"Yes, it is," Theo said as he stood to remove his sweatshirt. "Oh my gosh, I'm so embarrassed. I can't believe I left my hall monitor sash on. This is just one of the many things I have accomplished since being cured of my fears last summer. And yes, I said *HALL MONITOR*. That's right, guys, *an elected position.*"

"Theo, that is terribly impressive," Madeleine said genuinely. "Perhaps you can tell me about the campaign later."

"I bet you were the only one who wanted to do it," Lulu added under her breath.

"Well, that is an outright — well, not technically a lie, but definitely mean."

"OK, so you're a closet monitor, but what about your fears?" Mrs. Wellington asked.

"It's *hall* monitor, and my fears, well, they are doing *great*. I mean top notch — that's where I put my fears, on the top notch of my closet, which is in the hall that I monitor, because I am a *hall monitor,*" Theo said with a forced laugh before continuing. "Basically, I am a *free man.*"

"Am I to take your proclamation of being a *free man* to mean you no longer phone your family members every hour?"

"No way! I'm running around New York City,

43

catching buses, hopping on subways, eating at questionable establishments, and generally throwing caution to the wind—total renegade in glasses. That's actually my nickname on the street—the renegade in glasses who also happens to have been *elected* hall monitor. And for the record, even if no one runs against you, you are still considered an elected official."

"I don't know why you're so proud. It's not like anyone even *likes* elected officials," Lulu said honestly.

"That is not true. My father is very fond of the President...of the Elks Club, very fond," Theo shot back defensively.

"And what about the rest of you? Are you all *cured?* Madeleine?"

"As you can see, I am veil- and repellent-free. And while I certainly don't rejoice in spiders or insects, they no longer plague my every thought. It's behind me now, as is my need to prespray rooms, wash in boric acid, or use Wilbur the exterminator. I am rather proud to say that earlier this year, I even petted a...spider's... furry...belly...in Holland Park, simply as a leisure activity," Madeleine babbled awkwardly.

"Lulu?"

"Um, I take elevators and lock bathroom doors even when there aren't windows. I am one hundred percent cured. Can I go home now?"

"Oh, my little strawberry-blond parrot, you certainly haven't lost your spunk. Sporty?"

"Parrot?" Lulu mouthed to Theo before rolling her eyes.

"Oh, I'm Lulu, and my life is so hard because every-one gives me cute little nicknames even though I'm really mean," Theo delivered in a whiny female voice.

"Chubby, I believe I was speaking to Sporty, not you," Mrs. Wellington said as her lips dipped a shade darker. Due to oversized capillaries, Mrs. Wellington's lips darkened whenever she was embarrassed, irritated, or angry.

"Every morning I'm up at six to hit the beach for an hour, ride some waves, get in the zone," Garrison answered. "It's pretty awesome. I'm a beach bum; the water's my life now. So it's been cool to see you, but the waves are calling me, if you know what I mean."

"Well, I suppose I will have to let you go home, then.

And please don't worry about Schmidty, the animals, or myself—we'll manage somehow. Although it would have been so helpful to have all of your eyes and ears to help stop this beast from stealing my most prized possessions..."

"Oh dear," Madeleine said, gasping. "Has he taken family heirlooms?"

"Worse! My wigs! The burglar has stolen every single one of my wigs, except the one I'm wearing. Have you any idea how long it takes Mrs. Luigi to grow her hair to make one of my wigs? Three years! And it's not just the wigs; the burglar has also taken four crowns, six sashes, one plate of Casu Frazigu cookies, two framed pageant photos, four lipsticks, and a nail file. Soon there'll be nothing left but my bald head."

"Who would *want* that stuff?" Garrison asked.

"An old pageant rival dying to get revenge. Everyone knows a beauty queen is nothing without her hair."

"But aren't all your pageant rivals dead by now?" Theo wondered.

"I'll have you know, at least three of my rivals are still living...in nursing homes. And you would be surprised how fast they can move with a walker and a tank of oxygen. I've put Munchauser on the case. He's investigating the ladies; he sends updates weekly."

"I bet the guy in the forest is stealing your stuff. You know, Abernathy? Your greatest failure, the one student you couldn't help... blah blah blah," Lulu uttered in a bored tone.

"It *is* awfully suspicious that Abernathy always appears during the burglaries. But it's impossible. Abernathy simply couldn't be the thief—he's terrified to enter Summerstone," Mrs. Wellington said, rubbing her chin.

"I'm no Sherlock Holmes—although I think with a little training I could be—but it's obvious Abernathy is working in cahoots with someone. Come on, Mrs. Wellington, haven't you ever read Nancy Drew? I mean, we don't need CSI to solve this," Theo finished.

"Abernathy has never really had any friends. The likelihood of him finding an accomplice seems highly improbable. He lives in the Lost Forest. Who is he going to enlist, a squirrel?"

"Maybe not a squirrel, but you would be surprised

what raccoons can do," Theo said knowingly. "They have opposable thumbs and great night vision. Born burglars."

"Well, there you have it! The raccoons are behind it. Guess it's time for us to hit the road," Lulu said decisively.

"Yes, I suppose it is. But just one thing before you go," Mrs. Wellington said with a smirk.

CHAPTER 5

EVERYONE'S AFRAID OF SOMETHING:

Ornithophobia is the fear

of birds.

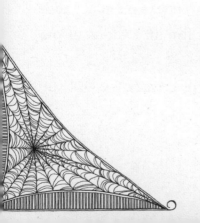
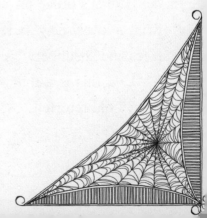

THE RENEGADE IN GLASSES

Schmidty, please get the lights," Mrs. Wellington said mischievously as she turned on the projector and clicked a slide into focus. "Here we have the lovely Miss Lulu Punchalower at twelve-thirty PM in the lobby of her dentist's office on Brystale Avenue. And may I add, what a lovely neighborhood you live in. I adore all the trees and shrubbery."

"Um, this is a total invasion of privacy. I could sue you," Lulu retorted.

"By all means. I believe you're acquainted with my attorney, Munchauser," Mrs. Wellington said icily as she held Lulu's stare.

"And here is Lulu again at one-ten PM, still waiting for someone '*to happen*' to ride the elevator with her, which, lucky for Lulu, finally occurs at one-thirty PM, making her only one hour late for the appointment. Then there are the fake trips to the restroom while out with her family..."

"Lulu, I'm horrified. Is nothing sacred?" Theo squawked, shaking his head.

"What? So maybe I like someone to accompany me when taking the elevator or entering small bathrooms with tricky locks. Big deal! I may not be totally cured, but *sort of cured* is more than enough to get me through life," Lulu said indignantly.

"Life is about more than just getting through, Lulu," Theo said poignantly. "I guess that's just another lesson *unelected* people don't understand."

"And now on to London..."

"Surely you didn't send someone all the way across the Atlantic to check in on me?" Madeleine asked

52

tensely. "Going through customs alone is such a headache, not to mention the currency exchange."

"Never underestimate a beauty queen with airline miles," Mrs. Wellington said with a snicker. "Madeleine, it appears that you have nearly emptied your piggy bank with under-the-table payments to Wilbur the exterminator."

"It is not a *piggy bank!* It's a travel fund."

"Oh, my apologies, dear. A travel fund is much more dignified to pilfer from in the name of bedroom exterminations and netting. Yes, dear girl, we have pictures of the veil you've been wearing to sleep, waking up early to take it off so your parents don't find out. Absolutely shameful."

"I cannot believe that you went to such lengths to check in on me. A letter would have sufficed," Madeleine said huffily to Mrs. Wellington.

"Am I to suppose that you would have given me an honest assessment? I don't think so."

"Oh, I tried, Mrs. Wellington! But there was an outbreak of mutant palmetto bugs in the United Kingdom, something to do with global warming..."

"Don't wait for retirement to save the environment," Theo proudly announced.

"They've been bombarding me with images on the telly. I couldn't take the chance of a mutant tiptoeing across my face at night with all my senses drowned in REM waves. The bugs could have laid eggs in my hair, my eyebrows—why, even on my eyelashes. I simply couldn't allow that to happen..." Madeleine trailed off before lowering her head in disgrace.

"Then there's...the surfer," Mrs. Wellington said, suspiciously eyeing Garrison.

"Yup, that's right. I'm a surfer. I love the water," Garrison offered in a cracking voice.

"Well, you do have the wet suit," Mrs. Wellington said while clicking a slide. "And the tan, and the—"

"Sorry to interrupt, but I have to say it. I think Garrison is too tanned. He clearly needs a refresher in the dangers of the sun," Theo said knowingly. "He'll be a raisin before he's thirty if he keeps this up. And friends don't let friends grow up to be raisins."

"As I was saying, Garrison," Mrs. Wellington continued, without any regard for Theo's comments, "you may have the tan and the board, but an actual surfer? No.

However, I give you credit—it certainly took a great deal of work to wake up, walk down to the beach, get all sandy, wet your hair in the public bathroom, then head to school."

"The public bathroom at the beach?" Theo murmured to himself in disgust. Just thinking about it made him want to take a bath in Purell.

"The currents are like arms pulling me in different directions. I only just learned to doggy-paddle in a pool. And all these storms make the water even choppier. Then there's tsunamis, and hurricanes, and floods—it's just too much! You can't tell anyone, please! It's my whole thing, Garrison the surfer. My dad's even stopped making fun of me. . . . I can't go back to that."

"You can't build a house on a rocky foundation," Theo said, shaking his head judgmentally at Garrison.

"Oh, what now—you're a construction worker?" Garrison mouthed off.

"Honestly, Theo, I have never seen you take such delight in others' misery. You ought to be ashamed of yourself," Madeleine stated emphatically.

Theo blanched, placing his left hand dramatically across his chest, clearly wounded by Madeleine's comments.

"And then there was Chubby."

"No need to waste your time on me. I've been a dream. Sure, there's the odd occasion I worry about something, but it's never anything irrational. Just everyday stuff like returning my library books on time, because let me tell you, that nickel a day can really add up."

"Chubby, I'm not even going to get into the horrible disguises you wore to spy on your family members or the reports you submitted to your parents on your siblings' outings."

"You can't tell them! They'll kill me! I only just convinced them the doorman was behind it. Sure, they've been pelting him with pickled eggs from the Korean deli, but he's a strong guy. He can take it."

"Not to worry, Chubby. I am far more interested in discussing your personal deforestation plan."

"Some environmentalist," Lulu scoffed.

"Um, Lulu, have you not heard my slogans? I am all about the environment," Theo said before turning toward Mrs. Wellington. "That whole tree thing was a simple misunderstanding. I thought the newscaster said *pine* flu. I mean who calls pigs *swine*? Why not call it pig flu? It's really the fault of those fancy-name-using newscasters."

"I think you need help," Lulu said to Theo, "and I don't mean that in a kind or caring way."

"Yes, well, he certainly isn't the only one, now, is he?" Mrs. Wellington snapped. "And what is this abomination of posture? Why, it's as if evolution never happened!"

The contestants immediately threw their shoulders back and sat straight as boards.

"Good," Mrs. Wellington said coolly. "Now that we have clarified the fact that you all *need* to be here, there is something I must ask you. Have any of you been careless and babbled to an outsider about our institution, inadvertently inspiring them to come and steal from me? Perhaps you remember speaking with a bald person desperately in need of some hair?"

Madeleine slowly raised her hand. "I am absolutely certain, that is, positively one hundred percent sure, that I did not speak to anyone regarding School of Fear. I told everyone that I spent the summer at a United Nations debate camp in New York."

Mrs. Wellington nodded, then turned toward Lulu.

"What!" Lulu said defensively in response to Mrs. Wellington's stare. "I told everyone I was in a juvenile detention center."

"A painfully plausible story," Mrs. Wellington said as she looked to Garrison.

"I didn't say anything. And as far as everyone in Florida is concerned, I was at surf camp in Hawaii last summer."

"And you, Chubby?" Mrs. Wellington said with a heavy dollop of doubt.

"It's in the vault, a place no one can access, not even me. Well, that's not entirely true, because it's *my* vault, but you know what I mean."

"No, Chubby, I'm afraid I don't," Mrs. Wellington said with darkening lips. "Please explain."

"Well, I had been planning on telling everyone I was on an archeological dig or at space camp or interning at the White House. Something really exciting, because that's what people have come to expect from me," Theo said haughtily. "But my derelict brother, whom I may add Lulu was instantly taken with, decided to tell everyone I was at fat camp instead."

"A most believable story. Please commend your derelict brother on my behalf," Mrs. Wellington said before rubbing her chin and furrowing her brow.

"Mrs. Wellington, a bit ago you mentioned Munchauser sending updates. Does this mean you finally receive post?" Madeleine asked excitedly.

"No, Miss Madeleine," Schmidty explained from the side of the room, "I'm afraid it's far more rudimentary than receiving mail. Munchauser calls a local boy with updates, which the boy then transcribes on a piece of paper before riding his bike to the base of Summerstone and dropping it in the letterbox. I then reel the box up using a dumbwaiter."

"That sounds *really simple;* I'm totally ditching my cell phone when I get home," Lulu said sarcastically. "Maybe I'll even look into getting a carrier pigeon."

"I feel the need to go on the record as saying that pigeons are not very clean, and I'm not just talking about bird flu, which, on an aside, is not as I previously thought, a bird with a runny nose and a cough. Pigeons have been known to carry everything from cryptococcosis to bedbugs," Theo said authoritatively as his stomach grumbled loudly. "I'm starving. When's lunch?"

"It's eleven AM, Theo," Lulu said, rolling her eyes.

"I hardly ate any breakfast. I'm trying to work on my portion control. But do you realize how small an actual portion of cereal is? It's, like, four cornflakes and half a raisin. Fine, a whole raisin. But that's not enough for a growing man!"

"Chubby, not to worry. We will have a proper lunch when the new contestant arrives," Mrs. Wellington announced casually.

CHAPTER 6

EVERYONE'S AFRAID OF SOMETHING:

Isolophobia is the fear

of being alone.

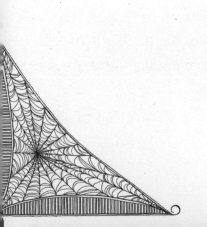
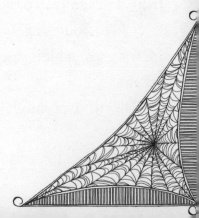

I think I'm going to cry today, because I am going away! I miss my mommy and daddy and they're right in front of me," a small girl sang off-key in the backseat of a Honda Civic as her parents in the front seat shook their heads in frustration.

"Child, your singing is pushing me to the brink of insanity," a middle-aged Indian man said in a thick accent.

"Daddy! I promise I won't sing for the rest of the

summer. Just let me stay with you! Please, Daddy! Please!"

"No, we can't. Your brothers and sisters have gone on strike. They say you take all our attention, twenty-four hours a day. You are the work of twenty children! This cannot go on!"

"Mommy, let's run away from Daddy. We can start a new life on a rice paddy!"

"We have been over this. This is for your own good as well as the good of the entire family. Don't you care about your brothers and sisters? Don't you want them to be happy?" the young girl's American mother asked from the passenger seat.

"Not if their happiness means my being alone."

"You won't be alone. You will be with a teacher and other students all summer."

"Fine…"

"And please try not to sing…"

Displeasure never displayed itself quite as overtly as it did on Lulu's face when she learned that another contestant was to join School of Fear. The young girl's cheeks had gone red and splotchy, but most notable were Lulu's hardened eyes, which she kept perfectly trained on Mrs. Wellington. Theo watched Lulu with a mixture of fear and admiration. He had never been able to scare anyone with a stare, or even with words, for that matter.

"Let's not get ahead of ourselves. Maybe Mrs. Wellington was talking about a new cat or dog," Theo whispered to Lulu from the side of his mouth.

Lulu momentarily broke her focus on Mrs. Wellington to assess what Theo had said. She had to admit it was a possibility.

"Are you talking about a new cat or dog or an animal of any kind?" Lulu asked Mrs. Wellington, her head cocked to the left.

Theo watched Mrs. Wellington intently, as if trying to will the old woman to say yes. Not only did he wish to appease Lulu, but he wasn't keen on a new student either.

"I am afraid not, Lulu. The new contestant is human, or so her parents claim. However, should the contestant surprise us with a fur coat and sharp teeth, Macaroni will be thrilled. He's been a bit lonely since those nutters down the street, the Knapps, have stopped letting Jeffrey come for playdates."

"No, thanks, Mrs. Wellington," Lulu interrupted. "This bunch of weirdos is more than enough for me. Let's return this new one. Get a refund. Store credit. I don't care, just send it away. Do whatever you need to do, but no new contestant."

"I've got to agree. What if it's another..." Garrison paused while looking at Theo.

"I hear you, Gary," Theo said obliviously. "Another Lulu would be rough on me too. Just might be the straw that broke the hall monitor's back."

"Enough with the Gary," Garrison snapped.

"A little aggressive for a surfer, don't you think?" Theo muttered under his breath.

"Perhaps we're being needlessly negative," Madeleine chimed in before Garrison could respond to Theo. "Maybe *he* will be a lovely addition to the group."

"It's a *she*, not a *he*," Mrs. Wellington corrected Madeleine.

"Oh, well, that is absolutely wonderful," Madeleine said meekly, while glancing over at Garrison.

It was a tad irrational and extremely overprotective, but Madeleine simply could not bear it if Garrison were taken with the new contestant. Why, it would be absolute torture! What if she were some beach-loving surfette? Madeleine knew it to be petty and wrong, but she said a silent prayer for the girl to be outrageously unattractive. Even as Madeleine thought it, she felt dreadful. It was such an un-Madeleine thing to wish, but crushes have been known to make girls go utterly batty.

As Mrs. Wellington expounded on the many virtues of having new energy at Summerstone, there was a knock at the door. Before anyone could answer, Schmidty entered with a petite young girl. Half Indian and half American, the girl had an utterly adorable face, complete with a toothy smile and matching dimples. Dressed in a blue pantsuit with a string of pearls and a briefcase, the child's style was a great deal more grown-up than her age.

"Schmidty, is this the housekeeper I ordered from the catalog? I must say, I had no idea they dressed them so professionally."

"Madame, you ordered a self-cleaning vacuum, not a

child laborer; those tend to be frowned upon in developed nations. This is Hyacinth Hicklebee-Riyatulle, our new student."

"I always wanted a hyphenated name. I even asked the tooth fairy for one, but alas, it never came," Mrs. Wellington said, stepping toward the smiling young girl. "Welcome to School of Fear."

"Oh my gosh, I am so super-duper excited to be here," Hyacinth said in a bubbly and overly energetic voice. "At first I thought, no way am I leaving my friends and family for the summer. But then my mom explained that I would be with other kids and you and Schmidty the whole time. And in truth, I had absolutely no choice in the matter since mom and dad said that if I didn't come here, they were going to drop me off on the side of a deserted highway. After that, I got really, really, really, really excited. So excited, in fact, that I wrote a song about it. Should I sing it? Does anyone have a harmonica handy? Mom didn't think I should bring mine."

"Uh," Mrs. Wellington uttered as she looked at the perplexed faces of Theo, Garrison, Lulu, and Madeleine.

"Perhaps we should save singing for the talent portion of the program. Now then, Hyacinth…"

"I prefer to go by Hyhy. All of my friends call me Hyhy, and I consider all of us friends, even though we haven't technically met. Oh my gosh, do you feel that? We're having an imaginary group hug from across the room."

"Yes, well, as long as we keep it imaginary, everything shall remain civilized," Mrs. Wellington said as she assessed the overactive young girl. "Why don't you let go of Schmidty's hand and take a seat?"

"OK. Can I hold your hand? I love holding hands. I feel really connected when I am holding someone's hand. And what's better than feeling connected to people?"

"Silence," Lulu muttered to herself before rolling her eyes. "Silence is definitely better."

Ignoring Hyacinth's request to hold her hand, Mrs. Wellington pointed to the desk in front of Theo, believing him to be most likely to embrace the chatty child. Hyacinth immediately pushed her desk between Theo's and Madeleine's as Garrison and Lulu watched in shock from behind.

"Hyacinth, you are new, so I shall overlook this infrac-tion, but I don't take kindly to contestants moving furniture."

"It's Hyhy, remember? And sorry. I just wanted to sit next to my new besties," Hyacinth said as she looked at Madeleine and Theo with a manic grin.

"I hate to be a stick-in-the-mud, but I'm feeling like this relationship is moving a bit fast for me," Theo said. "I don't even remember your last name, and you don't even know my first name, and already we're at bestie status. And truth be told, you're a little young for me. I mean, what are you, eight?"

"I'm ten, but I'm small for my age. I believe age is a mind-set; numbers don't really matter, so let's not let that stop our friendship."

"Well, I must agree with Hyacinth about age," Mrs. Wellington said seriously.

"Hyhy!" Hyacinth corrected Mrs. Wellington.

"Madame, when death is the next stage in life, age is more than a mind-set," Schmidty explained to Mrs. Wellington.

"I can't bear the idea of dying without my wigs! To

be buried with just one wig is too horrible. One must have options, even in death," Mrs. Wellington mumbled to Schmidty before returning her eyes to young Hyacinth.

Smiling widely, Hyacinth reached into her briefcase and pulled out a furry noodle-type creature on a leash.

"I really wish you had listened to me about returning her, Mrs. Wellington. She brought a rat on a leash," Lulu said disdainfully.

"Is he up-to-date on his rabies shots?" Theo yelped while pushing his chair away from Hyacinth. "Rats, like pigeons, carry a lot of diseases. Diseases that I don't have antibiotics for at this current time."

"Celery is a ferret, not a rat. And she is my absolute best friend, the bestie of all besties. Plus she's my official food taster," Hyacinth said with a smile. "Oh my gosh, the dog is totally giving Celery the eye. They're going to be such great friends!"

Macaroni was most definitely not giving Celery the eye or wishing to be her best friend. As a matter of fact, Macaroni didn't much care for animal friends anymore. The dog had been downright relieved when Jeffrey the poodle's parents, the Knapps, had a falling-out with Mrs. Wellington, bringing all canine playdates to an end. Apparently, the couple who insisted on wearing matching clothes at all times thought it negligent that Mrs. Wellington refused to get Macaroni braces to correct his underbite. Of course, one must remember that the Knapps pushed Jeffrey in a pram, fed him from a bottle, and burped him after meals.

Hyacinth dangled Celery in front of Macaroni in hopes of cementing the animal love connection as Madeleine watched in utter bewilderment.

"Pardon the personal question, Hyacinth, but are you a member of royalty?" Madeleine asked seriously.

"Oh my gosh! Do I seem like a princess?"

"No, not in the slightest, but members of royalty traditionally have used food tasters, which is why I inquired."

"Oh," Hyacinth said, nodding her head, "that makes total sense, but Celery tastes my food because I have a peanut allergy."

"Listen, I don't want to get off on the wrong foot, because we need both feet to walk." Theo awkwardly stumbled over his words. "But you didn't answer my rabies question. And I am sitting pretty close to you, so I think I have a right to know."

"You are so funny! Celery is up-to-date on all her shots. One day when you are giving a toast at my wedding, you'll be able to tell this story. Don't you just love making memories?"

"Is that what we're doing?" Theo asked. "Am I the only one who missed that?"

"You're ten and you're already talking about your wedding," Garrison said with surprise.

"Don't you wish there were friend weddings? Then we could all marry each other!" Hyacinth said with brimming enthusiasm as she looked from Theo to Madeleine to Lulu to Garrison.

"So, Hyacinth," Mrs. Wellington interrupted.

"Hyhy."

"Even her name annoys me," Lulu muttered to Garrison.

"Yes, of course, Hyhy, your terribly dignified nickname," Mrs. Wellington continued. "I would like to introduce you to Theo, fear of hidden dangers and/or death affecting either him or his family; Madeleine, fear of spiders and insects; Lulu, fear of confined spaces;

and Garrison, fear of water. Contestants, this is Hyacinth, fear of being alone."

"Oh, wait," Hyacinth said as she leaned her ear against the ferret's mouth before nodding her head multiple times. "Celery is feeling a little left out because you didn't introduce her to my new besties, and she is my original bestie, the best bestie!"

"Contestant," Mrs. Wellington admonished. "We may need to create a time limit for you when speaking, as I am quite sure I aged at least a year between all those besties. Now then, am I to presume that Celery the ferret speaks English?"

"I'm afraid not," Hyacinth said, shaking her head.

"Then how are you communicating with the animal?" Mrs. Wellington pressed on.

"I understand Ferret," Hyacinth responded confidently.

"You understand Ferret?" Mrs. Wellington asked incredulously.

"Yes, it's one of the many skills I bring to a friendship. I think that's why Celery and I are so popular. We have a lot to say between the two of us."

"Yes, we've noticed. I ought to tell you that I happen to speak Ferret fluently."

Hyacinth looked at Mrs. Wellington seriously before she again leaned in and listened to her ferret. "OK, this is really awkward for me, because you are my friend and Celery's my friend, and I don't want to get caught in the middle, but Celery says you're...lying."

"I happen to sit on the board of the North American Human Ferret Speakers. What does your ferret have to say about that?" Mrs. Wellington retorted.

"Wow, this is getting really intense for me. I hate being stuck between friends," Hyacinth said before turning toward Madeleine. "Mad Mad, I'm going to need to lean on you during this difficult time of being stuck between two friends in a snit."

"Mad Mad?" Madeleine repeated. "I'm terribly sorry, Hyacinth, but I prefer Madeleine or Maddie. And did you mean *lean on me* literally or figuratively? Not to be difficult, but if you meant that literally, perhaps you could put Celery down first. Not that I don't think she's absolutely charming—"

"Wait just a sec, Mad Mad," Hyacinth interrupted

as she again pressed her ear to Celery's mouth. "Mrs. Wellington, Celery wants me to tell you this, and it's really hard for me to do, but here it goes. Celery said there is no such thing as this Human Ferret Board."

"Does anyone else feel like they're stuck in a creepy cartoon?" Garrison asked seriously. "I always hated cartoons where animals talk...it's just not right."

"There's a whole lot of *not right* in this room," Lulu added as she watched Hyacinth again press Celery's mouth to her ear. "And I'm not even talking about the kid's pantsuit or briefcase."

"Celery is positive that you don't know how to speak Ferretish," Hyacinth retorted.

"It's called Ferretese. And I will show that dubious little rodent. *Chhjunnnnchhhhjunn,*" Mrs. Wellington chirped, while Theo, Madeleine, Lulu, and Garrison lowered their heads in shame. They each felt it was terribly undignified, even for Mrs. Wellington.

"Madame, I am loath to interrupt you when you are attempting to converse with a ferret in a made-up language, but I feel I must bring to your attention that you

76

are attempting to converse with a ferret in a made-up language. Perhaps it's time for a short break?" Schmidty asked while nudging Mrs. Wellington gently.

"Well, I could use a lip-gloss refresher and a spritz of perfume. I would love a wig change, but of course that is out of the question," Mrs. Wellington blustered as she exited the ballroom after Schmidty.

"So Mad Mad, Celery is dying to know whether you spell your name like the French cookie or like the girl in the book."

"I certainly am not trying to be cheeky, but did I mention that I prefer Madeleine or Maddie, but not Mad Mad?"

"What? No way. You can't be serious. Come on. I'm Hyhy. She's Lulu, you're Mad Mad, he's Gar Gar, and that's Thee Thee. You can't mess up the Five Friends Forever Group!"

"Bet Gary's sounding a whole lot better these days, Gar Gar," Theo said to Garrison with a smirk.

Garrison grunted loudly in frustration before running his hands through his blond locks. "No way, ferret girl. There is no way I am letting you call me Gar Gar or

Maddie Mad Mad or even Theo Thee Thee, although he may not mind. But there is definitely no Mad Mad or Gar Gar."

"Yeah, and there's no Five Friends Forever Group, we just met you, and you're younger than all of us, so if anyone's doing the whole group leader thing, it's not going to be you, got it?" Lulu said firmly.

Hyacinth nodded her head dramatically before once again pressing her ear to Celery's mouth. "Oh, no, Celery says you guys hate me," Hyacinth said before exploding into a loud wail. "You really hate me!"

"Hyacinth, we most certainly do not hate you. And I think perhaps it's best that you stop listening, or pretending to listen, or whatever it is you are doing with that ferret."

"Why are you yelling at me?" Hyacinth screamed at Madeleine between sobs.

"Yelling? I most certainly was not yelling at you. I only spoke loudly because you are crying at a very high decibel."

"Are you mad because the British Empire is over? Because I had nothing to do with that!"

"Pardon me? But are you totally bonkers? What on earth are you running on about the fall of the British Empire for?" Madeleine said forcefully.

"It's never a good sign when Maddie gets angry," Theo mumbled to no one in particular.

"Theo, now is hardly the time," Madeleine snapped.

"You are absolutely right, and I say that as a man with a sash." Theo paused before looking meaningfully at Hyacinth. "That's right, I'm an elected official."

Hyacinth again pushed Celery's face into her ear and nodded emotionally. "Celery says she's really surprised someone elected a marshmallow. That was Celery, not me, so please don't hate me, Thee Thee! Celery has always had a thing against chubby people. I think she's secretly afraid you'll sit on her. Oh, please! Please don't hate me!"

"Oh, yeah?" Theo said while looking the ferret square in the eye. "I may be a marshmallow, but I have a graham cracker," Theo said, pointing to Lulu, "a piece of chocolate," he continued, pointing to Garrison, "and a fire," he finished, pointing to Madeleine. "So I'm not just a marshmallow, I'm a s'more. And a s'more is more than you could ever be . . . ferret!"

"Theo," Lulu said with a sigh, "did you just tell the ferret off?"

"Your comebacks stink, Theo. Seriously, we need to work on that," Garrison said while pushing his blond mop from his face. "And I definitely wouldn't suggest bringing food into it.... Wait, is that Wellington?"

Garrison pointed to the far window, through which the students watched Mrs. Wellington, followed by Schmidty, followed by Macaroni, chasing a very dirty but quick Abernathy across the booby-trapped and obstacle-ridden lawn.

"I guess they caught him stealing something in the house," Garrison said with a shrug.

"If I remember correctly, Abernathy is afraid of coming into Summerstone," Madeleine said pensively.

"Then maybe he was stealing lawn furniture for his crib in the forest," Theo added sincerely.

"*His crib?* You think the forest dweller has a crib?" Lulu said in disbelief to Theo.

"I think that dirty man is giving us the gift of friendship," Hyacinth said with a massive smile.

"That is the one thing I am pretty sure he's *not* doing," Lulu said firmly.

"He's distracting Mrs. Wellington and Schmidty so that we have time to bond. That spells friendship to me. As a matter of fact, I am so touched I think I may have to sing. *Thank you, dirty man, I'm your new biggest fan; let's go out and get a tan, maybe even an electric fan…*"

"Wait. Pantsuit may be on to something," Lulu said seriously.

"I'm sorry to be the Simon Cowell of the group, but that was awful," Theo said with a terribly guilty expression. "She's not on to anything, not even the school glee club, and their standards aren't very high."

"Not the singing!" Lulu said as she quickly rose from her chair. "Abernathy…he's the distraction for the burglar."

"We need to search the house!" Garrison said, realizing his leadership skills were needed as he headed toward the Great Hall.

"Maybe we should just wait here. After all, we are not trained crime fighters," Theo said with a strange mixture of nervousness and guilt.

"Theo," Madeleine snapped, "we can't just sit by and let them steal Mrs. Wellington's valuables. Think of all she did for us last summer! And think of all she'll do for

81

us this summer if this burglar doesn't drive her too batty!"

"Fine," Theo relented. "A hall monitor's work is never done."

"Don't leave me! Please! Wait for me!" Hyacinth exploded as she took off after the others.

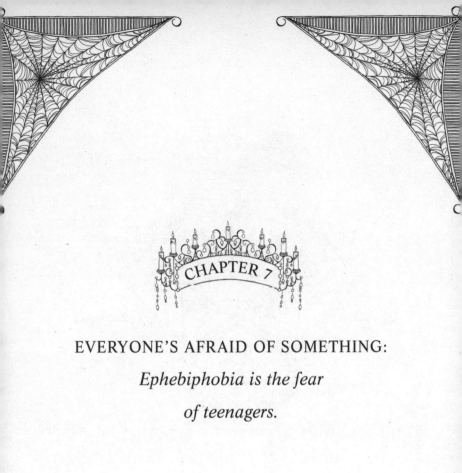

CHAPTER 7

EVERYONE'S AFRAID OF SOMETHING:

Ephebiphobia is the fear

of teenagers.

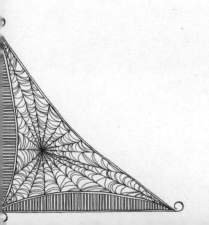
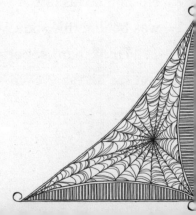

Following what proved to be an unsuccessful search for the burglar, Mrs. Wellington, with her makeup partially melted off, paced in front of Schmidty, Macaroni, Theo, Lulu, Garrison, Madeleine, and Hyacinth. Her mind was fast at work, desperate to figure out who was behind this audacious break-in.

"Think hard, Sporty," Mrs. Wellington said. "Did you see his face? Even just a glimpse?"

"We're all assuming it's a man, but who's to say it's not a woman?" Lulu asked.

"In an unscientific survey that I conducted in a dream, I statistically proved that more men are criminals than women," Mrs. Wellington asserted before focusing on Garrison again.

"Honestly, I was too far away," Garrison said, "and he was covered in black, like a bodysuit."

"So you're saying he's a dancer? Any particular movement? Ballet? Modern?"

"It wasn't like he stopped to tap-dance along the way. All I know is he was wearing a black bodysuit."

"I'm sweating just thinking about it," Theo said seriously. "He must have gotten a terrible heat rash. I hope he's got calamine lotion at home, or at the very least preparations for an oatmeal bath."

Hyacinth suddenly started crying, much to the shock of everyone around her.

"Why are you crying? Are you frightened?" Mrs. Wellington asked sympathetically. "Or are you worried the burglar did in fact develop a heat rash?"

"Neither," Hyacinth whimpered. "Celery thinks the other kids hate me just because I'm new."

Mrs. Wellington stared at Lulu, Theo, Garrison, and Madeleine with crimson lips. Much as she had when teaching the art of smiling and waving, Mrs. Wellington barked her orders.

"Tell her that she is mistaken! Tell her that you're all friends!"

"We don't hate you, just your ferret. Really, we're friends," the foursome droned unemotionally to a now-smiling Hyacinth.

"Besties?" Hyacinth asked in a chipper tone.

Mrs. Wellington shot each of the students a firm glance.

"Sure," Theo said reticently.

"Of course," Madeleine mumbled.

"Uh-huh," Garrison grunted.

"Whatever," Lulu said with a roll of the eyes and a sigh.

"I am so happy I'm going to sing a song," Hyacinth bubbled. *"Hyhy wanted to cry cry, when she heard you all were saying bye bye, but now she knows it was just a lie lie, so she can let out a big sigh sigh!"*

"I may have misspoken when I referred to singing as your *talent*," Mrs. Wellington said as she femininely perched her right hand on her hip. "But we will have to address that later, as we have a terribly busy day. Contestants, before lunch, why don't you take Hyacinth upstairs," Mrs. Wellington said calmly.

"She's not rooming with us, is she?" Lulu asked, pointing her head in Hyacinth's direction.

"Of course I am. It's going to be like one big slumber party all summer. Celery and I are so excited. We even brought extra barrettes so we can all braid each other's hair before bed."

"OK, this is School of Fear, not Barbie's Band Camp. There will be no braiding of the hair or pillow fights or late-night gab sessions or singing along with the Jonas Brothers," Lulu said, laying down the law.

"I wouldn't mind singing some Jonas Brothers before bed," Theo said sincerely to Lulu, before realizing again that perhaps this wasn't the best time.

Hyacinth turned her head toward Celery, who was perched precariously on her shoulder, and once more pretended to listen.

"Celery says you're going to change your mind as soon as you see how much fun Mad Mad and I are having. Oh, and that she thinks your new nickname should be Carrot, because then we'd have Celery and Carrot."

"Don't call me Carrot. And you look like a pirate with that ferret on your shoulder," Lulu said disdainfully.

"Oh my gosh! Celery and I are obsessed with pirates. Only we wish they'd get better clothes. Why does everything have to be so drab? What's wrong with a nice pantsuit?"

"I am impressed by this little one; taking insults as compliments is quite a skill," Theo said knowingly to the group. "A lot of people don't realize that."

"Thank you for that stimulating discussion, Chubby. And Lulu, you needn't worry; we have placed her in the extra bedroom across from the barbershop," Mrs. Wellington explained.

"I don't remember a room being there," Garrison said suspiciously.

"Madame has me wallpaper over doors when rooms are out of service," Schmidty intoned.

"Yeah, that makes sense," Lulu deadpanned. "Why close a door when you can spend the day wallpapering over it?"

"Contestants, please see Hyacinth—"

"Hyhy," Hyacinth corrected.

"Please see Hyhy to her room so Schmidty can prepare lunch."

"Fine, let's go," Lulu begrudgingly acquiesced.

"Lulu, can I hold your hand?" Hyacinth asked with a huge smile.

"That is a really bad idea," Garrison informed Hyacinth. "I think Theo's a better bet."

Hyacinth placed Celery on the floor before grabbing Theo's hand excitedly.

"I really hope you're an avid hand washer or Purell user," Theo mumbled to Hyacinth.

"Oh my gosh! How fun is this?" Hyacinth said to Theo animatedly. "Yet another memory for your wedding toast."

"You do realize the legal age for marrying in the United States is eighteen, right?" Theo responded. "And don't get any ideas about me, OK? I'm not letting someone lock me down until I'm at least thirty. I'm quite the catch back home, just so you know."

"Yeah, he's the renegade in glasses," Lulu said sarcastically as she led the group upstairs.

The extra room, as Mrs. Wellington referred to it, was actually labeled that on its door. There was a small black-and-white sign hanging from the dark wooden door that read THE EXTRA ROOM.

"So here is your room, Hyhy. Our rooms, as you probably saw, are at the start of the hall," Lulu explained as she flung open the door, revealing a small, quaint room with black-and-white tartan wallpaper and a green paisley bedspread.

"Well, it's fine for my luggage to be in here, but I'll be staying with you and Mad Mad."

"No way," Lulu responded.

"Yes way! Yes way! Yes way! Yes way!" Hyacinth chanted back.

"Perhaps we can discuss this later, Lulu," Madeleine interjected. "For now, Hyhy, why don't you unpack, and we will be right down the hall."

"Why don't we unpack together? It will be such a great memory for us to share!"

"I'm pretty sure I'm speaking for the whole group when I say that I would rather not have that memory," Lulu explained before turning and walking toward the girls' room.

"Yeah, we'll see you in a minute. Seriously, it's no big deal," Garrison seconded as he took off after Lulu.

"Mad Mad?" Hyacinth asked in a slightly desperate tone.

"What's that you say, Garrison?" Madeleine asked as she took off down the hall at warp speed, leaving Theo all alone, with Hyacinth holding his hand.

"So?" Theo said awkwardly.

"I'm so glad we're besties."

"Let's not rush into anything, OK?"

Hyacinth laughed as she pulled Theo into her room.

"Oh my God! Celery!" Theo screamed as he pointed to the ferret on the floor. "She's choking on a... croissant!"

Without fully comprehending what Theo had said, Hyacinth bent down to check on her leashed ferret. With only a split second to escape, Theo took off down the hall, running faster than he ever had. By the time he made it into the girls' room, locking the door behind him, he was nearly asthmatic.

"Lo...ck...the...ba...th...room!" Theo panted to Madeleine, Garrison, and Lulu as he stood with his back against the door, scanning the room as he attempted to catch his breath. It was exactly as he remembered it: pale pink walls with white polka dots, portraits of cats in tutus, fuchsia curtains, mauve carpet, and cherry-colored paisley duvets.

From the hall Hyacinth pounded on the door, hysterically wailing.

"Theo, what on earth happened out there?" Madeleine asked.

"She sounds like a sea lion," Garrison added.

"I had to run. It was my only way out. She was holding my hand with some sort of steel grip. She may not look it, but I think she's a bodybuilder."

"A ten-year-old bodybuilder? Please," Lulu scoffed.

"Maybe extraordinary hand strength is the result of some exotic disease she caught from that ferret. Am I the only one who thinks her behavior is screaming Discovery Channel?"

"Yeah, she is a total freak. I mean, she's making me rethink all the mean things I said about you, Theo," Lulu agreed. "And that says something, because I said a lot, like more than I can even count."

"You really need to work on your compliments, Lulu."

"And what on earth was she doing bringing up the

British Empire? As if I'm proud of the British occupation of foreign lands. Hardly! But you certainly can't hold me responsible. I wasn't even alive. Why, my mother wasn't even alive!"

"Yeah! Your grandma wasn't even alive!"

"Well, actually no, Theo. She was alive. That's why I stopped with my mother."

"Ah, it's all coming together for me now."

"She's just so annoying and unchill." Garrison paused to think. "She's the total antisurfer."

"Um, you've never even surfed," Lulu pointed out.

"That doesn't mean I don't know the mind-set; it's all about being Zen, cool, one with the water."

"LET ME IN!" Hyacinth screamed as she attempted to ram the door open with her small body.

"Not to distract from the child attempting to knock down the door behind me, but does Mrs. Wellington really know how to talk to ferrets?"

"Theo, she's a weirdo, but she's no Dr. Doolittle. That was pageantry at its best," Lulu said confidently.

"I'm not sure; I mean, she did train the cats. I wouldn't put it past her to have found some way to communicate with ferrets," Madeleine said sincerely.

"Maddie's right. When it comes to Wellington, we never know," Garrison said as he watched the door jostle within its frame.

"I thought we were besties! Is this a test? Are you testing me? Please, I love you guys! Celery says she hates you, but I don't! I forgive you for abandoning me in the hall! Please, just come out!"

"Get a grip, kid!" Lulu hollered through the door. "We're coming out in a second, just chill, OK?"

"OK! Sure! Just come out soon," Hyacinth whined. "Hurry!"

"I'm not going out there first," Theo whispered to the others. "My hand is still cramping from that death grip she had it in."

"Fine, Theo. I'll go out first, give you some time to massage your hand, maybe soak it in hot water," Lulu said sarcastically as she opened the door.

Much to Lulu's surprise, the hallway was empty. After all the fanfare and hysterics, the child had disappeared. Lulu couldn't say she was disappointed. On the contrary, she was extremely relieved. She had been more than a little worried that Hyacinth was going to try to hold her hand, or worse, hug her.

Lulu didn't smell or hear anything—it was a silent, odorless offense, but a rather gross one nonetheless. It wasn't until the infraction had seeped through her shirt, wetting her shoulder, that Lulu realized something had landed on her. Something very earthy; it was green and runny and about the size of a quarter.

CHAPTER 8

EVERYONE'S AFRAID OF SOMETHING:

Chiroptophobia is the fear

of being touched.

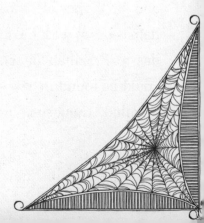

Lulu slowly rolled her head back, nervous about what she would find. If she hadn't been at Summerstone, she might not have given the greenish blob a second thought. But this was, after all, a residence with a B and B, a special "inn" dedicated to creatures whose names begin with the letter *B*. Everything from barracudas to Brazilian biter snakes to bees to Bombay bats could be found in Mrs. Wellington's B and B. With that in mind, Lulu swallowed hard and forced herself to look. What she saw was nothing short of a Cirque du Soleil performance. Hyacinth was hanging precariously upside down from the chandelier, with the ferret perched on her arm.

"Was that ferret poop?" Lulu screamed as Hyacinth and Celery dropped from the chandelier, pinning the irate girl to the floor.

Hearing the ruckus, Madeleine, Garrison, and Theo rushed into the hallway.

"Oh Lulu, I've missed you sooo much!" Hyacinth howled as she hugged the furious strawberry-blond girl. "Let's tie our wrists together so we're never separated again!"

"Get off me!" a red-faced Lulu hollered. "Get off me right now!"

"Don't leave me!" Hyacinth whimpered intensely. "We're besties forever! Besties in this life and the next!"

"Wow, she really expects a commitment. I don't even know if I believe in the afterlife, and she's already confirming friendships. I've always admired planners," Theo said to Madeleine and Garrison.

"Help me!" Lulu yelled. "Get this thing off me!"

"Lulu and Hyhy have merged into one, never to be undone! It's going to be so much fun," Hyacinth sang in her usual flat tone.

"I think we're going to have to pull Hyacinth off Lulu," Garrison said to Madeleine.

"Perhaps Theo could aid you in that, seeing as he's a boy. You must admit it does seem a more gentlemanly role."

"Could somebody just help me!" Lulu screamed.

Madeleine and Garrison both turned to Theo, who frowned awkwardly.

"I can't. My hand is still in recovery."

After a few sighs and shakes of their heads, Madeleine and Garrison lifted Hyacinth and Celery off Lulu. The small child wiggled and flipped her body around as they yanked her away. Within seconds a smiling Hyacinth had fastened herself to Garrison's arm.

Unmoved by Hyacinth's sweet expression, Lulu pulled herself off the floor with steely-eyed focus and walked right up to the petite child. "First your ferret pooped on me, and then you pinned me to the floor. What is wrong with you? This is not cool, do you understand that?"

"I am so sorry that Celery pooped on you. But Celery

wants me to tell you that she's not sorry, because apparently she doesn't like you, since you abandoned me in the hallway. However, it was pretty traumatic for me seeing a bestie get pooped on by another bestie. But you should know, Celery eats only organic food."

"Wow, what a relief! Because that's what I was worried about, whether your ferret ate organically or not," Lulu said, groaning.

"Lulu, go change your shirt for lunch," Garrison said, before looking down at Hyacinth, still attached to his arm. "What were you doing hanging from the chandelier?"

"Celery was changing a lightbulb," Hyacinth said slowly.

"That's so thoughtful," Theo said genuinely. "I didn't even know ferrets could change lightbulbs. Raccoons, sure, but ferrets, who knew?"

"Theo, I highly doubt she's serious," Madeleine interjected. "Now we ought to get downstairs. It's almost lunchtime, and you know how Macaroni hates to be kept waiting..."

"He's not the only one. I am *starving*," Theo said, leading the procession to the dining room.

Madeleine trailed Theo in a state of total irritation. She knew Garrison couldn't stand the aggravating child, but she couldn't help feeling envious. Oh, how Madeleine would love to walk arm in arm with Garrison. Simply thinking about it made the girl blush.

Mrs. Wellington, Schmidty, and Macaroni were seated at the formal dining room table, which was covered in pink lace, dusty candelabras, and rose-patterned china. Three paintings of English bulldogs, Macaroni's predecessors, hung from the mint green walls.

"My apologies," Madeleine said politely upon entering the dining room, "but we had a slight incident with Hyacinth."

Garrison led Hyacinth to the chair next to Theo and gently nudged her to take a seat, much to Theo's displeasure.

"Gee, Gary, you sure you don't want to keep Hyhy next to you for lunch?"

"No, that's all right. I don't want to be greedy."

Hyacinth immediately pulled her chair right next to Theo's and smiled brightly. She then placed Celery on her shoulder and leaned toward the ferret. "Mad Mad?" Hyacinth called kindly across the table. "Celery wanted me to thank you for throwing us under the bus for being late to lunch."

"I'd be careful, or I may throw your ferret under an actual bus," Lulu said with a glare as she took the seat across from Hyacinth.

Hyacinth again leaned toward her ferret and listened. Without any warning she stood, grabbed her plate full of food, and smashed it on the floor.

"Sandwich killer," Theo whispered as he inched away.

"How dare you?" Mrs. Wellington wailed. "That china is older than Schmidty!"

"Celery made me do it," Hyacinth offered meekly. "She thinks Lulu poisoned our food."

"Wow, that sounds a lot like a Theo story," Lulu interjected.

"In other words," Garrison explained, "totally made up."

"Let the record show, I take offense at that," Theo said indignantly.

"What is this record you keep referring to?" Madeleine wondered aloud.

"Hyacinth, you are a most insufferable child. Now sit

down," Mrs. Wellington said with crimson lips. "I was already at my wits' end with those annoying Knapps, leaving flyers for canine acupuncture in the letterbox. And now you've robbed me of owning a complete set of china. You are not to be trusted with any more dishes; you will simply have to eat off the tablecloth from now on."

"Hasn't Mrs. Wellington suffered enough? She's down to her last wig, and now she doesn't have a complete set of china," Theo murmured to Hyacinth.

"Absolutely appalling behavior," Madeleine seconded angrily.

"Celery made me do it. It wasn't my fault," Hyacinth shamefacedly responded.

"Now for Grace," Mrs. Wellington said as she reached for the centerpiece. But to her shock and dismay, the shell of Grace the turtle was missing. In honor of her having once saved Schmidty's life, all residents of Summerstone knocked on Grace's shell three times before eating.

"The burglar has taken Grace," Mrs. Wellington mumbled as she stood up from the table.

"I've lost my appetite," Schmidty babbled with

tear-filled eyes as he waddled out of the dining room after Mrs. Wellington.

Without any regard for the emotional upheaval, Hyacinth began feeding Celery, who was perched on her shoulder. Rather surprisingly, the ferret easily ate off a fork and even closed her mouth while chewing.

"If I ever develop an allergy, I am going to make Macaroni my food tester," Theo said while watching the ferret chew delicately. "But I'm not going to let him sit on my shoulder."

"If I may inquire, how, precisely, did you train Celery to alert you to peanut products?" Madeleine asked sensibly.

"Well, it turns out she's deathly allergic to peanuts, so if she dies, I'll know there's peanuts in there."

"What kind of a pet owner are you?" Theo screamed. "Someone call PETA!"

"It's a dangerous job, but someone's got to do it..."

"Does Celery know she has this job? Because from the looks of it, I'm pretty sure she just thinks she's a pet," an agitated Theo said, embracing his role as animal protector.

Hyacinth yet again leaned toward Celery and listened,

or pretended to listen, or whatever it was that she was doing.

"Celery says she is aware of the danger, but she's up for the challenge, because I am her number one bestie. She also wanted me to tell you that she is sorry she called you a marshmallow, and that she thanks you for looking out for her."

"Well, I am a hall monitor. It's a rough gig, but as the principal says, I'm the only *man* for the job."

"The only *boy* for the job," Lulu interjected loudly.

"In Judaism a boy becomes a man at thirteen, and I am thirteen, Lulu."

"Yes, but you're not Jewish."

"Yet! I haven't decided on any one religion as of now. I'm keeping my options open, so if you'll excuse me, I am in the middle of taking a compliment from a ferret."

"Fine. We can discuss your potential conversion to Judaism later, but I should tell you that if you're planning on having a bar mitzvah, I'm not getting you a gift."

"Lulu," Madeleine asked, "is that really necessary?"

"Fine, Theo, I'll get you a gift."

"Celery doesn't think you should invite Lulu to your hypothetical bar mitzvah."

"Tell your ferret to sleep with one eye open," Lulu snapped back at Hyacinth.

"She always does. That way she can alert me if someone tries to leave the room while I am sleeping."

"I'm awfully sorry, but I do not believe that it is possible for a ferret to sleep with one eye open," Madeleine said firmly.

Hyacinth again leaned toward Celery, nodding her head every few seconds.

"Celery says that just because you have an accent doesn't mean you have a veterinary degree, so back off."

"Your ferret could use a lesson in manners," Madeleine responded harshly.

CHAPTER 9

EVERYONE'S AFRAID OF SOMETHING:

Blennophobia is the fear

of slime.

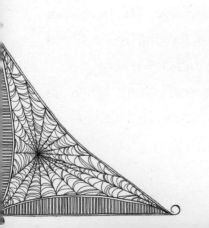
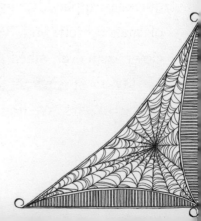

Mrs. Wellington and Schmidty somberly returned to the dining room as the children chatted over the remnants of lunch. The old woman resumed her place at the head of the table, whereupon Schmidty quickly reapplied her lipstick and rouge. The fresh coat of makeup left Mrs. Wellington looking more like a clown than ever, albeit a terribly sad clown.

"My most sincere apologies for exiting lunch so abruptly," Mrs. Wellington said solemnly. "The loss of

Grace greatly disturbed me. I can't help but wonder what's next? Stealing my false eyelashes? I will not allow it! We must fight this evil force! We must band together as an army!"

"Mrs. Wellington, I hate to interrupt, but I think you should know I'm a pacifist. That means no military organizations for me," Theo explained. "However, I am open to joining a *posse,* especially if there are matching jackets involved."

"Yes," Hyacinth squealed, "we should totally get matching jackets. And let's start a scrapbook/yearbook for all the memories we're making."

"Do I look like the scrapbook type?" Lulu responded wryly.

"Contestants, whether it be for an army or a posse, we must be strong. We must face our fears, if only to save me and my worldly possessions. So reapply your lipstick, we're going to the Fearnasium," Mrs. Wellington announced stoically before exiting the dining room.

"My mum prefers I not wear lipstick for another two years, so perhaps I'll apply lip gloss or ChapStick," Madeleine said to Schmidty and her fellow students.

"Do you have any flavored ChapSticks?" Theo asked. "Maybe cherry or root beer?"

"Theo, it's not food," Lulu snapped. "You can't eat it."

"Celery is feeling left out because she doesn't have any lips," Hyacinth said glumly. "Maybe we can apply eye shadow instead?"

"I believe it best we call off the makeup," Schmidty declared as he headed toward the Great Hall. "Once a ferret is in eye shadow, we're only one small step away from Macaroni in false eyelashes and rouge. And frankly, last time that occurred, he wasn't himself for days after."

Lulu, Madeleine, Garrison, and Theo, with Hyacinth attached to Theo's arm, followed shortly thereafter. Mrs. Wellington sauntered femininely down the Great Hall, keeping in perfect synch with the ticking of the pocket watch embedded in the floor. She stopped in front of the faded plywood door to the Fearnasium and began fiddling with its lock.

"There is no greater preparation for any army than mental preparation," Mrs. Wellington asserted as she spun the combination dial.

"I thought we agreed to call it a *posse*," Theo interjected.

"Yes, of course, the posse."

"Madame is never so flexible with me," Schmidty said sulkily.

"Sometimes it takes a man with a sash—a hall monitor, to be exact—to lay down the law," Theo boasted while puffing out his chest.

"I'd like to call for a moratorium on Theo discussing being a hall monitor, effective immediately, to last for the remainder of his life, or at the very least *my* life," Lulu stated loudly to the group.

"Joke all you want to, Lulu, but we both know that with the first sign of trouble, you're going to call—"

"Garrison," Madeleine interrupted. "Sorry, Theo, but I think we can all agree that Garrison is far calmer under pressure and a great deal braver than you are. But please believe me, if I ever wanted to make a sandwich, you would be my first call."

"Finally," Mrs. Wellington mumbled as she opened the door. "Welcome back to the Fearnasium, a gym for exercising your fears."

The vast room roughly measured the dimensions of

half a basketball court and was packed with contraptions, dentist's chairs, coffins, needles, tombstones, puppets, and so much more. After decades of use, the Fearnasium was rather well stocked with the objects of nearly every childhood phobia imaginable. And if additional information were needed, there was always the Fearclopedia, a wall of leather-bound books spanning the spectrum from Aeronausiphobia to Zeusophobia.

"After me, contestants," Mrs. Wellington announced as she led the pack past an aquarium holding tiger sharks, taxidermied owls, and miniature trolls in clear little plastic bags.

"I would just like to remind everyone that *there's nothing fantastic about using plastic,*" Theo said as he pointed to the heap of plastic-encased trolls.

"Your slogans suck," Lulu moaned.

"Hey, Lulu, why so hostile? I'm not the enemy. Carbon footprints are the enemy."

Before Lulu could respond, a graveyard of antique porcelain dolls silenced her with their cracked faces, missing eyes, and chipped paint. As Madeleine, Theo, Hyacinth, Garrison, and Lulu moved, they felt a multitude of beady black eyes following them, while an up-tempo song wafted through the air. The computer-generated music sounded much like the theme song to *The Price Is Right.*

"Welcome to *What's the Worst That Could Happen?*" Mrs. Wellington proudly announced as the group rounded a corner to see a bright and shimmering stage come into view. Bulbs flickered and flashed in a million colors as the music grew louder and Mrs. Wellington grabbed a microphone.

"Contestants, please take the stage," Mrs. Wellington beamed manically into the microphone.

Overstimulated by the loud music and flashing lights, Hyacinth ran onto the stage and began jumping up and down. With her fists pumping and legs kicking, she was quite a sight. Even Celery appeared alarmed.

"I've never been on TV before!" Hyacinth screeched as Madeleine, Theo, Garrison, and Lulu took their places behind the row of podiums.

"Before we start today's game of *What's the Worst That Could Happen?*, I'd like to thank our studio sponsor—me. So thank you, me!" Mrs. Wellington belted out in a loud and overly confident tone. "And remember, only speak when spoken to, and always speak when spoken to! Heeerrrrre we go!"

"From the great state of Rhode Island, we have Miss Lulu Punchalower," Mrs. Wellington said with her strange game-show-host inflection.

"And?"

"And, Lulu, we would like to know, what's the worst that could happen if you were trapped in a bathroom without any windows?"

Lulu stared at Mrs. Wellington as small balls of spit exploded from her overly pink mouth. "Um, I guess I would yell and scream and bang on the door until someone heard me."

"That's it?"

"Well, I'd be freaking out too. My left eye would throb and my chest would tighten…"

"But you wouldn't suddenly be drenched in curdled milk?"

"What? No!" Lulu quipped as a cascade of sour lumpy milk splashed down on her. "That smell," Lulu said, gagging.

Mrs. Wellington quickly hit an obnoxious buzzer.

"Remember, contestant, only speak when spoken to, unless you want more milk. And now, on to contestant Theo Bartholomew, from the great city of New York!"

Theo froze, unnerved by the sight and stench of Lulu.

"So, Theo, we would like to know, what's the worst that could happen if you didn't spy on your brothers and sisters?"

"Oh, I don't know. Maybe injury, arrest, even death!" Theo theatrically shot back.

"Yes, well, those things could happen even with you watching them. We want to know what's the worst thing that could happen to *you* if you couldn't watch them."

"Well, I would probably age at least two years in the course of one night, just from all my worrying."

"But you wouldn't be pelted with moldy cheese?"

Theo braced himself for the onslaught of moldy cheese but it didn't come, much to Lulu's annoyance. The girl was covered in two-week-old milk and was adamant that the others suffer similar fates.

"No, I don't think that seems very likely, unless we were at an old-cheese warehouse," Theo said calmly.

"And what about being splattered in fish oil?"

As Theo's lips formed a response, thick and smelly oil washed over him.

"But I'm a vegetarian!" Theo protested as Mrs. Wellington turned to Madeleine.

"And now, from all the way across the pond, Madeleine Masterson, we would like to know what's the worst that could happen if a spider sat next to you on a bench?"

"Well, I would grow terribly tense and nauseous, and then my skin would crawl as I fought the urge to vomit."

"But even if you did in fact vomit, you wouldn't be doused in honey and feathers?" Mrs. Wellington asked as a crude mix of honey and chicken feathers covered the young girl.

Garrison and Hyacinth, both tense with anticipation, surveyed the messy and smelly fates of their peers.

"Hyacinth, the youngest member of the group, from downtown Kansas City, we would like to know, what's the worst that could happen if you were left alone?"

"Well, I would cry and feel really scared and disoriented."

"But you wouldn't be soaked in day-old bathwater, would you?"

Hyacinth, with Celery on her shoulder, closed her eyes as the brown water cascaded over her small body.

After Garrison was creamed by a puree of moldy peaches, the filthy, sticky, stinky, moldy fivesome, all of whom had indeed experienced the worst that could happen to them, were hosed down outside and sent for showers.

CHAPTER 10

EVERYONE'S AFRAID OF SOMETHING:

Somniphobia is the fear

of sleep.

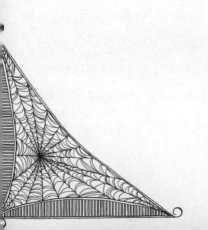

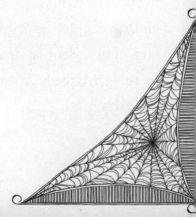

FERRETTTS

Dinner was an awfully mild-mannered affair compared to lunch. There was no plate smashing or messages from Celery. The long and arduous day had depleted everyone both mentally and physically, resulting in little to no conversation at dinner. And when Hyacinth requested that Mrs. Wellington force Madeleine and Lulu to let her sleep in their room, the old woman merely shrugged. Apparently she too was more than a tad exhausted.

Garrison, Theo, and a pajama-clad Macaroni fell fast asleep within five minutes of returning to their room. Theo didn't even bother to do his usual mental goodnight to his parents and siblings. Tonight he simply closed his eyes and snuggled up to the snoring bulldog.

Unfortunately, the girls were not so efficient in falling asleep. But one must remember that they had both Hyacinth and Celery to contend with. The prospect of sleeping alone in her room had pushed Hyacinth into a state of absolute hysterics.

"Please," Hyacinth said with big buglike eyes as she dropped to her knees in front of Lulu, "just let me sleep on the floor. You won't even know I'm here. Celery and I don't snore or talk in our sleep. We're so quiet we're almost invisible."

"No way, kid. I have had more than enough of you and that ferret today."

"Lulu, perhaps we're being a tad harsh," Madeleine said. "She *is* only ten."

"Yeah, I'm only ten and I'm immature for my age, so really it's like I'm eight. Who would make an eight-year-old sleep alone in a strange old house while a burglar is on the loose and that other weird guy, Abernathy..."

"Lulu," Madeleine said firmly, "we simply cannot leave her alone."

"Fine," Lulu acquiesced. "You can sleep in the doorway. That way, if the burglar comes back, he'll trip over you first."

"Lulu, is that morally correct?" Madeleine protested. "Using a child as our alarm system?"

"It's totally fine. We're in the gray area between right and wrong. Nothing to worry about, Maddie, I promise."

Hyacinth and Celery laid their pink sleeping bag in front of the door as Madeleine put on her night veil and crawled into bed. Lulu watched Madeleine closely, remembering the days when she insisted on wearing the veil everywhere. They really had come a long way since last summer. Perhaps there was something to Mrs. Wellington's methods after all.

Early the next morning, Theo cracked open his sleepy brown eyes, unsure exactly what was happening. He couldn't put his finger on it, but something was terribly wrong. He attempted to call for Garrison, but he couldn't. There appeared to be something wedged in his mouth. Theo's mind immediately jumped to the burglar.

Was it possible that he had been tied up without ever waking? But wait, his arms and legs were wholly unrestrained. Theo lifted his left arm slowly off the bed. His stomach began to rumble as his hand neared his mouth. As Theo's fingertips grazed something rough, similar to a wool sock, the boy began to perspire. He started to pull the object out of his mouth. Seconds later, he recognized what it was—a ferret.

Theo sat up as he dragged Celery's head across his lips. With tears in his eyes he looked at the ferret's face and tried to scream, but Celery had left far too much fur in his mouth, silencing his bloodcurdling howl. As Celery scampered off Theo's bed, the disturbed boy turned to Garrison, who was still conked out. Deciding that Madeleine and Lulu would be more helpful, he dashed through the bathroom into the girls' room. Lulu and Madeleine were both fast asleep when Theo barged in.

"Help! Help!" Theo groaned hoarsely. "I think I have ferretitis!"

"Theo, what is happening?" Madeleine said groggily as she sat up in bed. "And what is that on my foot?" she screeched, throwing back the covers. It was none other than Hyacinth Hicklebee-Riyatulle.

"Morning, Mad Mad!"

"Good morning, Hyacinth. Would you mind terribly explaining why you are in my bed?"

"I'm pretty sure my question takes precedence, Maddie!" Theo said firmly. "Why did I wake up with your ferret in my mouth?"

"Wow, that is...hard-core," Lulu stammered while pushing the hair out of her face.

"Celery sometimes does that when she's cold. I sleep with my mouth closed, so it's not a problem for me."

"I can already feel the ferretitis taking over," Theo moaned as he grabbed his throat. "I could go at any second. Honestly, I'm a little surprised I'm still here."

"Ugh, Theo. You just made that disease up," Lulu said as she rolled her sleepy eyes.

"I did," Theo admitted, "but only as a placeholder until I get to the bottom of my symptoms."

"Symptoms?" Madeleine asked. "You look fine. And Hyacinth already told us Celery is up-to-date on her shots."

"Hyhy," Hyacinth corrected Madeleine before continuing. "Don't worry, Theo, after Celery was kidnapped by this crazy kid in my class and ransomed for my cheese sandwich, I decided it was probably a good idea for her to get all her shots again."

"I'm kind of craving a cheese sandwich; that can't be good!" Theo screeched.

"Theo, you always crave sandwiches. The only person who thinks about food more than you is Macaroni," Lulu responded. "And he's an English bulldog. It's in their genes."

With fear in his eyes and a touch of fur still in his mouth, Theo ran out of the room, down the hall, and past a bald, pajama-clad Mrs. Wellington on the staircase.

"Where on earth are you running off to, Chubby? Breakfast won't be ready for another half hour."

Theo ignored Mrs. Wellington as he took two stairs at a time. Through the foyer and Great Hall he ran, until he finally reached the kitchen. The boy dramatically dropped to his knees on the pink linoleum floor next to Macaroni. "Schmidty, I contracted something from that ferret, you know, the one with the gray fur?"

"Mister Theo, to my knowledge there is only one ferret at Summerstone, so yes, I know exactly of whom you're speaking."

"That mean girl—and I'm not talking about Lulu, who does occasionally punch me while claiming to fist-bump me..."

"Perhaps it's time to look into new friends, Mister Theo."

"I'm dying, Schmidty! Dying! I don't have time to make new friends. As it is, I don't know what kind of turnout my funeral will have. It's summer vacation, everyone will be out of town. Oh no, a bad funeral. That's even worse than a bad birthday party. Thank heavens I have a big family," Theo wailed. "And you'll come, right? I can count on you, Schmidty."

"Dear Mister Theo, the likelihood that I'll outlive you is about a billion to one."

"Well, so are the odds of getting ferretitis from a ferret sleeping in your mouth. That's right! That awful little ferret crawled into my mouth and slept in there. And *he* let it happen," Theo said angrily as he pointed to Macaroni. "He was next to me snoring and occasionally even releasing gas, and he never bothered to wake me and say, 'Hey, friend, there's a ferret in your mouth.'"

"Macaroni has never been much of a watchdog. Although technically, that's exactly what he does. He watches things happen but never feels the need to get involved."

"And to think I was going to give you a pawdicure today," Theo admonished Macaroni. "I was planning on a light pink nail polish that would go very well with your fur coat. But you can forget it. And if I die, don't even *think* about missing my funeral, Macaroni!"

"Will you be giving everyone a pedicure today?" Schmidty asked with excitement.

"*Schm,* you know I love you, but I've seen your toes," Theo said as he remembered Schmidty's jagged brown toenails. "You need professional help."

"Don't we all, Mister Theo."

"*Ahhhhhhh!!!!!!!!*" Hyacinth bellowed from upstairs, sending a jolt through Theo, Schmidty, and Macaroni.

"Oh, dear," Schmidty said as he headed for the Great Hall.

"Where are you going, Schmidty? I've got ferretitis! Have mercy on the young and plump!"

As if there were not enough happening, Mrs. Wellington's voice suddenly whipped through the Great Hall. "Schmidty! Get the tutu! We must leave immediately!"

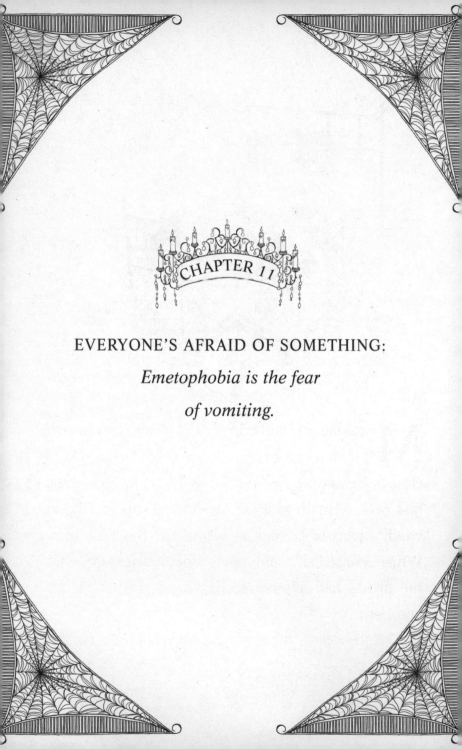

CHAPTER 11

EVERYONE'S AFRAID OF SOMETHING:

Emetophobia is the fear

of vomiting.

Madeleine was still rather tired when Theo ran off in search of a ferretitis vaccine, so she decided to close her eyes once again. Prior to Theo's intrusion, she had been mentally gallivanting through the small and windy streets of London in her smart school uniform. While Madeleine could not properly articulate why, the dream had left her feeling more than a smidge homesick.

The past year had been Madeleine's happiest. For the

first time, she had a true social life, chock-full of slumber parties, afternoon teas, and jaunts to Kensington High Street. Before plummeting into utter nostalgia, Madeleine reminded herself of the things London lacked, most notably consistent sunshine and Garrison. It was the thought of Garrison that prompted the young girl to crack open her eyes once again.

Seconds passed as Madeleine squinted, desperate for her eyes to focus properly. After years of imagining she saw spiders everywhere, the girl had become rather adept at refocusing. Only in this case, she couldn't shake the image of a spider. And for a very good reason—it was in fact a spider. A mere two inches from Madeleine's face dangled a large brown-and-burgundy spider. She wanted to scream, but she feared Hyacinth, who was still sleeping at her feet, would move abruptly. Madeleine was keenly aware that any quick movements could lead to a skin-to-furry-skin encounter.

Madeleine closed her eyes one last time, in a desperate bid to make the spider disappear. As she silently prayed, Madeleine felt a thump on the bed. She opened her eyes slowly, half hoping it had all been a dream. But the spider was still there, only now he had a very large friend with him. (Madeleine always assumed spiders were male. She quite honestly considered them too ghastly to be female.) Perched next to Madeleine's face, Errol the cat watched the spider with a sort of deranged reverence. It was awfully hard to work out whether Errol yearned to eat the spider or sit down for a chat. With an indecipherable gleam in his eyes, Errol slowly wrapped the spider around his paw, all the while dangling the creature precariously over Madeleine's face.

Madeleine's life, at least as far as she was concerned, was hanging on a cat's whim. And as everyone knows, cats are terribly unreliable. Why, it's entirely normal for a cat to stop midmeal, midplay, midnap, for a tongue bath. What if Errol did that right now? The cat would drop the substantial-sized spider on her face! It was almost too much for Madeleine to comprehend. As her stomach growled loudly, Madeleine pushed her body against the mattress with all her might. However irrationally, Madeleine hoped the mattress would swallow her whole. But of course that did not happen. Instead, Errol, still dangling the spider over Madeleine's face, took a seat on her chest.

With adrenaline pumping through her body,

Madeleine bounced up, pushing both Errol and the spider into the air. What happened next would replay for years to come in Madeleine's impressionable mind. As the pink-pajama-clad girl started for the door, Errol's tentative grasp on the spider broke. The cat jutted his legs out and puffed up his fur as he went sailing toward Hyacinth, still asleep on Madeleine's bed. Errol smashed into Hyacinth's chest, prompting her to scream as she jolted straight up. Meanwhile, the brown-and-burgundy spider spiraled through the air, landing on Madeleine's forehead. In that millisecond, Madeleine did not think. She did not reason. She simply slapped herself in the head. And this wasn't a light slap; this was a force of nature. So strong was the strike that Madeleine actually suffered a moderate case of whiplash.

"No!" Lulu screamed as she leapt out of bed and ran toward a dazed-looking Madeleine.

Sadly, Lulu was too late; far, far too late. Madeleine's dainty alabaster forehead was covered in spider road-kill. Amid a good deal of spider intestines and goo were the creature's thick and furry legs.

"Lulu," Madeleine said weakly, "it's not...is it? I imagined all that. I must have been dreaming, right?"

"Maddie, I want you to stay calm. Everything is going to be OK. I'm just going to grab a tissue..."

"God save the Queen," Madeleine mumbled as she simultaneously threw up and fainted.

Madeleine awoke to more than a mess; she awoke to a crime scene. Looking up from her bed, she saw a crowd of familiar faces displaying both concern and nausea. Her cheeks burned with embarrassment as she noted the pungent smell of vomit in the air. Everyone continued to talk loudly while Madeleine furiously tried to comprehend the events that had taken place. How was it possible that such a spider found her? Was it simply bad luck, or could it be something more sinister? Madeleine focused on Hyacinth, who was now dressed in a purple pantsuit. Did the peculiar little girl have it in her? As much as Madeleine yearned for someone to blame, she simply didn't think the ten-year-old could have done it.

"Maddie, you're awake," Garrison said sweetly, lifting her weakened spirits.

"Where did it come from?" Madeleine asked meekly as she sat up in bed.

"There's no easy way to say this," Mrs. Wellington muttered awkwardly.

"Please tell me, Mrs. Wellington," Madeleine pleaded as her heart rate jumped rapidly, "please."

"We were burglarized again last night..."

"Oh, well, I'm sorry," Madeleine said with immense relief, having thought the bad news was spider-related.

"And while stealing two of my portraits, the burglar also managed to knock over quite a few things."

"Oh, how dreadful. Does Schmidty need help tidying up?"

"No, dear, although it's terribly kind of you to offer, especially since Schmidty is not the housekeeper he once was—"

"Madame," Schmidty interrupted, "I implore you to remain on topic."

"Oh, yes, of course. Anyway, while rummaging through the house, the burglar got into quite a few jars in the B and B. Not all the compartments in the B and B were opened, thank heavens, or we would have a few Bermuda pythons on our hands. However..."

"Oh, dear, this is not the making of good news," Madeleine said as day-old food rose in her throat.

"The burglar tipped over the double *B*'s and the triple *B*'s."

"I know I am going to regret asking this," Madeleine said before swallowing loudly, "but what are the double and triple *B*'s?"

"Maddie," Garrison said calmly, "sometimes ignorance really is bliss."

"Yeah, I got to go with Gary on this one," Theo blurted out. "I really don't think you want to know."

"Celery thinks you should find out, but I don't," Hyacinth said with a smile. "And by the way, I had so much fun sleeping next to your feet last night. And FYI, they don't smell at all."

"This is hardly the occasion, Hyacinth," Madeleine said sternly.

Normally Theo would have rejoiced in Madeleine telling someone else that it wasn't the time. However, he was far too concerned about Madeleine's mental state to celebrate.

"Guys, let's get real about the situation; she's going to find out one way or another. At least this way she's prepared," Lulu said firmly.

"Please, you must tell me."

"The triple *B*'s are the Balinese Brown and Burgundy spiders. You already seem to be rather well acquainted with them," Mrs. Wellington said with a wry smile. "And the double *B*'s are the Bulgarian beetles. But no need to worry, neither is poisonous. As a matter of fact, the beetles are heralded for their intellect in Eastern Europe."

"How many of these horrid creatures are on the loose?" Madeleine whispered hysterically.

"One hundred of each," Mrs. Wellington said as she winced with anticipation.

"*Ahhhh!!!!!!!!!!!!!!*" Madeleine hollered, opening her mouth wider than a hippopotamus's.

"I'm pretty sure I saw her tonsils," Theo murmured to Hyacinth as he leaned away from Madeleine's deafening shriek.

"Don't mention tonsils in front of Celery; she gets superjealous that she doesn't have any. Celery really wanted to have them removed so she could sit around and eat ice cream all day, so you can imagine how disappointed she was when she learned she didn't have any," Hyacinth whispered back.

Theo merely nodded his head in response to Hyacinth's strange rant on ferret tonsils before focusing his attention back on Madeleine.

"Maddie, don't worry, I'm not going to let anything happen to you," Garrison said heroically.

"Garrison, how can you say that? You're not even a trained exterminator."

If Madeleine hadn't been so terrified, she might have found Garrison's pledge romantic in a *Gone With the Wind* sort of way. But she was far too preoccupied fighting the urge to vomit to bother blushing at Garrison's macho gesture.

"I can't stay here. Summerstone is a pit of spiders and beetles," Madeleine wailed. "Hundreds of spiders and beetles on the loose. Please, I can't bear it! Throw me out the window! Or just kill me! They could be anywhere! Absolutely anywhere! Wait! I think I feel something on my leg! What is it? Someone look! It's moving!" Madeleine screamed while flailing about on the bed.

"Miss Madeleine, we are to leave as soon as you're dressed. I'm afraid the bugs are only half the story," Schmidty announced glumly before turning his eyes to Mrs. Wellington.

"The burglar left us a rather disturbing note," Mrs. Wellington said, handing the letter to Madeleine.

Dear Mrs. Wellington,

*We know what you are doing. Meet us at 4 PM
to face the consequences. If you don't show up,
we will tell everyone the truth about what you've
been doing up there on the hill. And if you do
show up, we'll probably still tell everyone, but at
least you'll have a chance to defend yourself to
your peers.*

*The pageant starts at 4 PM sharp at Franklin
Park in Boston.*

All the best,
The Burglar

"I found it on my desk in the classroom this morning," Mrs. Wellington said. "Clearly it's from an old beauty queen looking for a rematch."

"I'm a little surprised the burglar signed it 'All the best.' How many thieves are that polite?" Theo asked the group.

"I bet Munchauser's behind this," Lulu said confidently. "He is a gambling addict, after all. He probably got in too deep at the racetrack and is looking for stuff to pawn."

"While it's true that Munchauser once lost his daughter in a game of poker, his cat in a game of chess, and his great-aunty Bertha in a game of blackjack," said Mrs. Wellington, "I certainly don't think he would ever steal from me. Actually, on second thought, I could imagine him lifting a few dollars here and there, but my wigs? Grace's shell? No, I don't believe it."

"We really must go if we are to make it to Boston in time," Schmidty stated emphatically.

"Yay!" Hyacinth exploded enthusiastically. "Road trip!"

CHAPTER 12

EVERYONE'S AFRAID OF SOMETHING:

Gerontophobia is the fear

of old people.

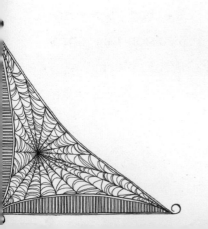

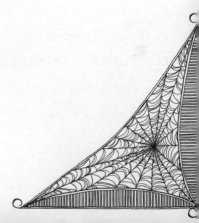

Madeleine sat sullenly on Summerstone's front porch, dressed in makeshift body armor consisting of a shower cap, her night veil, and an oversized plastic rain poncho. On her forehead was a rather large silhouette of the eight-legged beast she had vigorously demolished. So detailed was the impression that Theo could actually see the minute hairs on the spider's legs.

"Theo, tell me the truth—it's ghastly, isn't it?" Madeleine said in a nervous manner.

"Oh, no," Theo responded quickly, "you hardly notice it, except when looking at your face…"

"Theo!" Lulu yelled. "What is wrong with you?"

"Sorry! I hadn't thought out my lie, and then I became mesmerized by the detail of the imprint, and the next thing you know, I'm telling the truth. I think that spider may have hypnotic powers…so don't blame me…for the insensitive thing I said…" Theo trailed off as Hyacinth shoved her ear against Celery's mouth.

"Theo, Celery wants to know what's next. Are you planning to ask Madeleine about her crooked English teeth? Basically Celery thinks you are a superrude marshmallow," Hyacinth uttered with a smile.

"Excuse me, but my teeth are perfectly straight," Madeleine corrected Hyacinth before opening her mouth wide.

"But you're English, aren't you?"

"Yes, of course I am."

"Celery thought all English people had bad teeth," Hyacinth muttered. "Sorry. You know how ferrets can be, always believing stereotypes. Honestly, I have no idea where she picks this stuff up."

Luckily for Celery, Madeleine was too worried about the spider imprint to bother with the prejudiced ferret.

"You don't think it will scar, do you? I must get fringe immediately."

"Fringe?" Theo asked.

"Bangs to you Americans," Madeleine explained. "I can't spend my life looking at a spider imprint on my own head. Can you imagine anything worse?"

"Oh, I could *definitely* imagine something worse, but then again, that's my personality."

Lulu and Garrison stared at Theo with frustration. The boy lacked all social graces.

"That was a rhetorical question, wasn't it?" he said. "I really hate those."

Theo and Hyacinth were nominated to keep Madeleine calm while Lulu and Garrison checked on Mrs. Wellington and Schmidty, who were packing the essentials for the journey to Boston. Madeleine didn't care that they were going to Boston; she only cared that she was leaving Summerstone. This was especially true now that she had convinced herself that the spiders and beetles were crossbreeding. The girl was absolutely certain

...rs or spidles would be hatching any sec-
...ow.

Lulu and Garrison stormed into the foyer, eyes rapidly scanning the walls for spiders or beetles. Initially Summerstone's interior appeared utterly devoid of both the furry-legged beasts and their hard-shelled friends. It was only after Lulu noticed an earring moving on one of the pageant photos that she realized the enormity of the situation. Two beetles had rather astutely hidden in plain sight, each suctioning itself to Mrs. Wellington's photographed earlobes. How the beetles knew to do such things could be explained in only one way: the Bulgarian beetles really were the intellectuals of the Tenebrionidae family.

"There's a couple of beetles on the pageant photos," Lulu said, moving closer to Garrison.

"Look at the hydrangeas."

"They're smarter than we are, or at least smarter than Theo," Lulu said softly as she noticed a brown-and-burgundy spider crawling out from under the flowers.

"Contestants!" Mrs. Wellington shouted while running down the stairs in a fluffy pink tutu. "We haven't a second to spare if we're going to make it on time."

Schmidty, with a valise in hand, waddled quickly after Mrs. Wellington. Oddly, the old man didn't seem the slightest bit surprised or embarrassed by the tutu ensemble.

"I hate to be an ageist," Lulu said, surveying Mrs. Wellington's ridiculous ballerina getup, "but you are way, way, way too old to wear that. So let's spare that second and change this outfit. Stat."

"Oh, don't be a pageant Neanderthal, Lulu. I've won more titles in this tutu than I can count. Now really, we must hurry. And Schmidty, don't forget Macaroni and the gun."

"Wait a minute. What are we doing, exactly? Because I don't think Theo's going to be cool with a gun. And frankly, neither am I," Garrison added. "Surfers are all about peace, remember?"

"Mister Garrison, it's a flare gun, to signal the sheriff to get us at the bottom of the hill," Schmidty said as he flung open Summerstone's heavy front door. "We haven't time to dawdle. Hurry!"

Mrs. Wellington, Schmidty, Macaroni, Lulu, Garrison, Madeleine, Theo, and Hyacinth ran toward Summerstone's Vertical Tram.

"Schmidty, are we sure the SVT can handle all our weight?" Theo asked. "Because now we've got Wellington, Hyacinth, and that ferret. And in all honesty, I may have put on an extra pound or two in the last couple of days."

"It's fine, Mister Theo. But we really must hurry."

"Are you all absolutely certain no spiders or beetles or crossbreeds escaped on you? Have you checked thoroughly, because should I find another bug on me, there really is no telling what I'll do," Madeleine stated theatrically.

Lulu smiled nervously at Madeleine before subtly patting down her strawberry-blond locks and checking her earlobes.

"I really hope someone brought snacks," Theo whined. "I tend to get cranky when traveling without food."

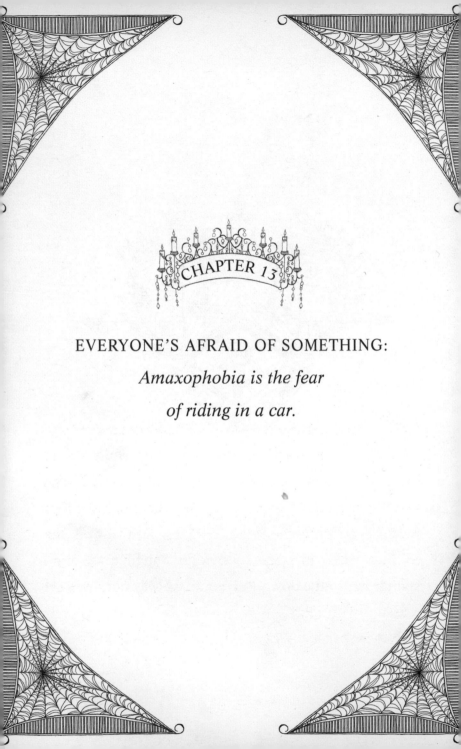

CHAPTER 13

EVERYONE'S AFRAID OF SOMETHING:

Amaxophobia is the fear

of riding in a car.

The sheriff, dressed in his khaki uniform and a large brown hat, leaned against a beat-up white van at the base of Summerstone. Until awfully recently, the van had been dragged up and down the mountain by a rickety wooden crane. Thankfully for all involved, the SVT was now in place. (Although watching the tram sputter and rattle down the mountain was not the most reassuring of sights.)

Not surprisingly, Lulu positioned herself to be first

off the tram. Once out, the young girl immediately hunched over to regain her composure. The ride down the mountain had been a long and painful affair. Never mind that it was only four minutes; it felt like hours to Lulu. As the young girl breathed deeply, Theo performed a series of stretches, much to the sheriff's amusement.

"My age is really starting to catch up with me," Theo said with a sigh. "I'm pretty sure I pulled a muscle on the ride down. Those little bumps against the mountain sure can hurt a man."

Unsure how to respond, the sheriff simply tipped his hat to the frenetically moving boy. Theo was instantly taken with the gesture and vowed to buy himself a wide-brimmed hat for the start of school. He imagined himself trolling the halls for hooligans, wearing not only his sash but a hat. And on the occasions when he passed a highly regarded teacher, he would tip that hat. The tipping of the hat seemed far more mysterious and cooler than the full-body hug, his usual manner of greeting people.

Schmidty, Macaroni, Hyacinth, and Celery were last to exit the SVT. Macaroni pulled hard on his leash in an attempt to get as far away as possible from Celery. The dog had developed a very understandable fear of ferrets after Celery had chewed one of his nails before climbing into Theo's mouth. Truth be told, so traumatic had the experience been that Macaroni was even looking at squirrels in a new light.

"Quick, Sheriff! We haven't time to chat," Mrs. Wellington insisted as she jumped into the front seat of the van.

"She could at least have asked; some of us may get carsick," Theo mumbled under his breath while getting into the backseat of the van. "Some people..."

As soon as the sheriff heard the last seat belt click, he started down the shadowy cobblestone road. The diverse assortment of passengers in the van fell into a peculiar silence. Perhaps it was the proximity of the forest, or the lack of light from the heavy growth of sticky vines, or even Macaroni's breath. Regardless of the cause, the only notable sound was that of the tires traversing the cobblestones.

The van rounded the last curve, bringing the edge of the forest into view. The sunlight burned bright outside the woods, creating an actual light at the end of the tunnel. As the van continued toward town, Theo cleared his throat loudly. After a few seconds the entire vanload, barring the sheriff, was looking at him with exasperation.

"Well, since I have your attention, I thought we could set a few ground rules," Theo said while attempting to pull his sash out from under his sweater.

"Stop moving, Theo." Garrison reprimanded the boy harshly.

"My apologies that you cannot see my hall monitor sash at the present time. As you may know, I am very focused on rules. Rules help everyone. Society needs rules, and so do we. Can we agree that rule number one is no fake dying?"

"Dying?" Hyacinth asked, intrigued.

"*Fake* dying," Theo corrected.

"Celery wants to know who is going to fake die."

"Last summer Mrs. Wellington pretended to die, and I want to make sure that no one else is planning on having a fake death."

"So if you die, it won't be fake?" Hyacinth concluded.

"Exactly," Theo said quickly. "Wait, I am not dying."

Hyacinth then leaned toward the ferret and nodded her head a few times.

"Does Celery think I am going to die?"

Hyacinth merely smiled and shrugged her shoulders.

"Oh, no, is Celery psychic?"

"Theo, what is wrong with you?" Lulu said impatiently.

"Lulu, animals can sense these things. Must I remind you about the cat that lived in the nursing home? He went to the patients' beds a couple of hours before they died, and then he would just sit there and wait for them to pass. What if Celery is like that cat?"

"Let's think about this rationally. What are the odds that Celery is a psychic ferret who can predict your death?" Lulu said with a sneer. "I would say about one in a billion."

"I'm feeling a little dizzy," Theo said dramatically. "Maybe it's a brain tumor."

"Seriously, Theo, relax," Garrison added before shaking his head at the dramatic boy. "Maybe we need to add a rule about melodrama too..."

"I just remembered something...horrible. That cat...her name was Peanut Butter...like peanut butter on celery...do you see the connection? Two foods that go well together. This is a sign. I'm doomed."

"The cat's name was Oscar," Lulu said with annoyance. "Like Oscar Mayer hot dogs."

"Thank heavens I'm a vegetarian. No food symbolism there. Talk about a close call."

Bored by Theo's descent into madness, Hyacinth turned to look out the window. In the distance the roofs of the Main Street shops, the dome of the bus station, and clusters of houses could now be seen. The van sped past farmhouses and old barns before turning onto Farmington's idyllic Main Street. Much as one might expect from a postcard or propaganda film, families were strolling down Main Street licking ice cream cones and laughing. It was such a foreign sight to Hyacinth that she lifted Celery to the window. Of course, ferrets are not known for farsightedness, so Celery missed the entire thing.

The second the sheriff pulled up in front of the station, he nodded to Schmidty, took off his seat belt, and jumped out of the van. Even as he walked toward the station, he took the time to tip his hat to each passing family. Theo, of course, made a mental note of how well the hat gesture was received by the townsfolk.

Mrs. Wellington jumped into the driver's place as Schmidty zipped into the front passenger seat.

"Wait a second," Theo said loudly. "*You* are driving us to Boston?"

"Well, I certainly can't let Schmidty drive; his stomach won't fit behind the wheel."

"And he's legally blind," Lulu added.

"Oh, stop that. It's all in his head. Men at his age simply want the attention. There's absolutely nothing wrong with him except his comb-over."

"Why can't the sheriff drive us? He seems sane," Garrison asked.

"He's on duty. We can't have a law-abiding man in the car the way I need to drive."

"I am going to have a problem with any and all law-breaking activities," Theo protested. "In other words, the speed limit is to be followed. Drawing from my hall monitor experience, I suggest driving well *below* the speed limit. As I always say, *for a safe hall it's better to crawl.*"

"So these catchy slogans aren't just about the environment? Lucky us," Lulu said with an eye roll.

Showing an unusual amount of restraint, Theo ignored Lulu and continued on with Mrs. Wellington. "Just because it says sixty-five doesn't mean you have to

159

do sixty-five. Personally, I think twenty-five on a highway is an optimum speed. And I am more than happy to ride shotgun to make sure nothing gets out of control."

"How is it that I am stuck on a car trip with Theo *again?*" Lulu moaned loudly.

"Luck? Friendship? Perhaps a mixture of both?" Theo said sincerely.

"Chubby, you are to stay out of the front seat," Mrs. Wellington said with fire engine red lips. "I will have no delays on this journey, do you understand? I am about to face off with a rival, and not that I am worried I will lose, because, let's be honest, that's impossible," Mrs. Wellington said with mounting certainty. "But if we are late, this pageant prune will tell everyone about my school!"

"Fine, Mrs. Wellington, I will let go of the speed limit issue, but what about bathroom breaks? I was thinking every ten to fifteen minutes."

"Theo, there is no way you need the bathroom every ten to fifteen minutes, and if you do, we'll drop you at a doctor," Lulu said harshly. "Preferably a mean one."

"This is not about me; I am speaking as Macaroni's advocate."

"Let me guess: animal advocacy is part of your hall monitor duties," Lulu said sarcastically.

"Maybe," Theo lied unconvincingly.

"I can't believe how much fun we are having on our road trip," Hyacinth squealed. "I only wish we had a camera to document the good times."

As Lulu prepared to respond to Hyacinth, Mrs. Wellington revved the engine. Without checking her mirrors or looking behind her, she slammed her foot on the gas and careened into the street, filling the van with the smell of burnt rubber.

CHAPTER 14

EVERYONE'S AFRAID OF SOMETHING:

Neophobia is the fear

of anything new.

Time check?" Mrs. Wellington barked at Schmidty as she crossed two lanes of traffic without looking.

"You know when you're having a nightmare and you realize it's only a dream, and this sudden relief comes over you?" Theo whimpered. "I really want that to happen now."

"I said time check, Schmidty," Mrs. Wellington roared as she barreled down Highway 90 without any regard for staying in her lane.

"We have an hour, so Madame, might I ask you to refrain from driving in reverse on the road," Schmidty said as he gripped the dashboard with white knuckles. "And please try to stay within the lines, or at the very least near them."

"Is this how all Americans drive on the motorway?" Madeleine whined. "No wonder people complain about American tourists."

Mrs. Wellington weaved between two large trucks before hitting the brakes, then speeding up, then hitting the brakes again.

"Celery feels kind of carsick from all these maneuvers," Hyacinth announced.

"Celery's lucky we're still alive," Theo said, before wiping his sweaty brow and bursting into tears. "I don't want to die on an empty stomach!"

"Theo," Garrison said, leaning forward to grab his shoulders, "you need to calm down. You have your seat belt on, and the van has air bags. You'll definitely survive."

"Um, I think I speak for all of us when I say we want to do more than survive. We want to avoid an accident altogether. Do you hear me, old lady in the tutu?" Lulu screamed while covering her now throbbing left eye.

"Would it be terribly inconvenient to stop by a hardware store on the way to the pageant?" Madeleine asked. "I would love to get a proper veil and some repellents."

"Now is hardly the time," Theo said to Madeleine with immense satisfaction.

"Hey, Mrs. Wellington?" Garrison croaked as he watched the elderly woman apply lipstick in the rearview mirror. "I think you've forgotten something."

"What's that, Sporty?"

"That you're driving!"

"Oh, so I am," Mrs. Wellington said, grabbing the wheel and jerking it abruptly in the other direction.

The van weaved across numerous lanes of traffic, setting off a storm of honks and clouds of burning rubber. Cars literally came to a grinding halt as the van careened across the highway, perilously close to causing a pileup.

"*Ah!!!!!!!!!!!!!!!*" Theo yelled before putting his hands over his eyes.

"Isn't that polite, all these drivers making room for me? Oh, and a parade's coming!"

"Madame, I believe that's a police officer," intoned Schmidty.

"Oh, don't be silly, there's music."

"That's the siren."

"The what?"

"Pull over, Madame."

"We don't have time. We are in a terrible hurry. You *know* you can't be late to a pageant, especially when someone's blackmailing you."

"Yes, but I'm afraid we must make time or they may arrest us."

"Arrest us? Absolutely not. I refuse to have my mug shot taken when my wig is in such a state!"

"Madame," Schmidty pressed on firmly, "you must stop."

Mrs. Wellington sighed loudly before slamming on the brakes.

"Madame! No! You have to pull off the highway."

"Honestly, all these rules. It's a terrible headache of useless information. All you need to know is how to turn a key. The car does the rest."

"Oh, Madame," Schmidty said, shaking his head, "so much of your life is simply...inaccurate."

"We haven't time for compliments. Handle this man, and let's get on with it," Mrs. Wellington said as a highway patrolman knocked on her window.

"It's glass," Mrs. Wellington shouted. "You can't put your hand through it."

"Ma'am, I need you to roll down the window and hand me your license and registration."

"Of course," Mrs. Wellington said, turning to Schmidty. "Valise, please."

Mrs. Wellington riffled through stacks of papers and knickknacks before pulling out a large and weathered pink document.

"Here's my license, officer."

"Ma'am, this is a cosmetology license."

"That is most correct, but I must admit, I haven't done a facial in years, so if you'll excuse us, we really must get going."

The officer leaned back and looked into the van suspiciously.

"Ma'am, who do these children belong to?"

"Oh, who knows? I can hardly remember my own name, let alone their parents' names. Now, officer, if you'll excuse me, I am in a terrible rush to get to Boston

167

for a beauty contest, so I am sure you'll understand if we continue this chat later, perhaps someplace more civilized, like at my mansion."

"Ma'am, I'm going to have to bring you in."

"In where? Are you trying to recruit me for the highway patrol? It simply won't work out; I've never looked good in khaki. Perhaps you can call me when you get some pink or lavender uniforms."

"Ma'am, I am arresting you."

"Don't be ridiculous. Call the governor; he knows me very well."

"Sure," the officer said sarcastically, "and then I'll call the president."

"Oh, please don't. His wife gets so jealous."

"Ma'am, I'm arresting you."

"Oh, very well. Call the president. See if I care."

"I need everyone to step out of the van."

The ride to the police station was rather dull, except of course for Mrs. Wellington's constant insistence on calling the governor. Once at the station, Mrs. Wellington and Schmidty were placed in a small holding cell while the children were taken into an office to be questioned.

At a round table, Theo, Lulu, Garrison, Madeleine,

and Hyacinth were seated uncomfortably before a large one-way mirror.

"Theo, Celery doesn't want you to mention getting arrested in the wedding toast. I don't care, of course, but you know Celery…so conservative," Hyacinth babbled nervously. "Although if I were ever going to be arrested, I would want it to be with my besties! Oh my gosh, we're besties behind bars!"

Ignoring Hyacinth's comments, Theo started walking around the small room. "All I can say is thank heavens I caught that *Law & Order* marathon, or I'd be pretty freaked out."

"We almost crashed a hundred times on the highway, we're in a police station waiting to be questioned, and we're late for a beauty pageant where one of Mrs. Wellington's rivals may out the school. How is this my life?" Garrison asked, throwing his hands up in the air.

"I feel the answer to that question may take longer than we really have time for here. Do you mind if we come back to that?" Theo asked earnestly.

As Garrison shook his head at Theo, a large and intimidating female police officer entered the room with a tray of candy and a really big smile.

"Hi, guys. How's everyone doing today?" she asked as she pulled out a chair. "I'm Officer Patty, and I'm going to ask you a few questions. But first, does anyone want any candy?"

"I do!" Theo said quickly.

"Didn't your mother teach you not to take candy from strangers?" Lulu asked severely.

"Weren't you listening? Her name's Officer Patty, so she's hardly a stranger."

"A stranger is someone you don't know, and we don't know Officer Patty, so put down the chocolate bar."

Theo's face was racked with misery and torment as he dropped the chocolate bar back on the tray. After all the shenanigans and near-death experiences on the road, he could really have used a sugar rush.

"I'm a police officer. You can trust me," Officer Patty said with a smile toward Theo. "Now, who wants to tell me what happened?"

"Hello, Officer Patty," Theo began. "My name is... Th—Hank...yes, my name is Thank...like Thank you...my parents are big on politeness. I would really appreciate it if we could not do the whole fingerprinting thing or mug shot...I really want to keep this out of the school paper if possible…could make reelection pretty tough…"

"Thank," Lulu said, "she's not arresting you, so you can relax. Your hall monitor status is safe."

"It's true, Officer Patty, I'm one of yours…a fellow badge-carrying…well, actually, mine is more of a sash, but—"

"Thank? Maybe you could stop talking for a second?" Lulu interrupted. "Officer Patty, we need to be released and so does Mrs. Wellington."

"About this Mrs. Wellington," Officer Patty said as she pulled out a notebook. "Who exactly is she?"

"She's our—"

"Don't say it!" Madeleine interrupted.

"She's our camp counselor," Lulu finished.

"Yes, she's our camp counselor!" Madeleine seconded enthusiastically.

"What's the name of this camp?" Officer Patty asked doubtfully.

"Camp Theo," Theo said with a huge smile.

"Camp Theo? I've never heard of it."

"Oh, yes, it's a small little place in the woods where everyone hugs hello, the kitchen never closes," Theo said with a reflective expression, "and there's always a choc-olate on your pillow."

"That sounds like *sooo* much fun!" Hyacinth added.

Nearby Mrs. Wellington and Schmidty sat in a small and dingy holding cell. Mrs. Wellington held her nose as Schmidty attempted to fan the area in front of her face. Two officers sat on the other side of the bars staring at the odd pair, much as one would watch animals at the zoo.

"Excuse me, young men, but I must get out of here. There is something extremely important happening today, and I haven't the time to be arrested. Couldn't we reschedule this whole thing for a later date? I could even bring tea sandwiches and pastries."

"Lady, you are a real piece of work," one officer said, shaking his head in disbelief. In all his years as a cop, he had never dealt with a woman in a tutu, let alone one accompanied by a man with the most elaborate comb-over in New England.

"Fine, I'll bring donuts," Mrs. Wellington said huffily. "Now can we postpone this incarceration nonsense?"

"If I may interrupt, officer, aren't we entitled to a phone call?" Schmidty asked calmly.

"Yeah, the law says you get one phone call," the officer answered, bringing the phone to the bars. "You better hope they're home, because I'm not feeling too generous today."

"Thank heavens, you've watched enough movies to know our rights," Mrs. Wellington said to Schmidty as she dialed.

Mrs. Wellington removed her pink rhinestone clip-on earring and pressed the old black phone to her ear. With a tight chest, she looked at the clock and saw that time was running out. As the old woman's blood pressure skyrocketed, she closed her eyes and said a silent prayer for the situation to be remedied.

"Hello? Munchauser?" Mrs. Wellington spat into the phone. "I've been arrested and I'm late for a pageant to meet the burglar...oh, it's a long story...call the governor and remind him where he would be without me... no, that was the president...the governor was afraid of being abducted by UFOs...who is Dawn Delight...are you at the track...you have five minutes to fix this or you're fired...oh, and I'll take twenty on Dawn Delight."

Exactly four minutes and twenty-eight seconds later,

the phone rang. The first officer rubbed his head as he listened. Then he passed the phone to another officer, who listened and nodded before passing the phone to yet another officer. The third and final officer mumbled something into the phone before slamming it down.

The clank of the receiver on its plastic frame brought Mrs. Wellington to her knees—quite literally. The old woman's knees actually gave out from shock as she slumped onto the sullied concrete floor.

"We're finished," Mrs. Wellington muttered as she lowered her head. "We'll never make the pageant in time."

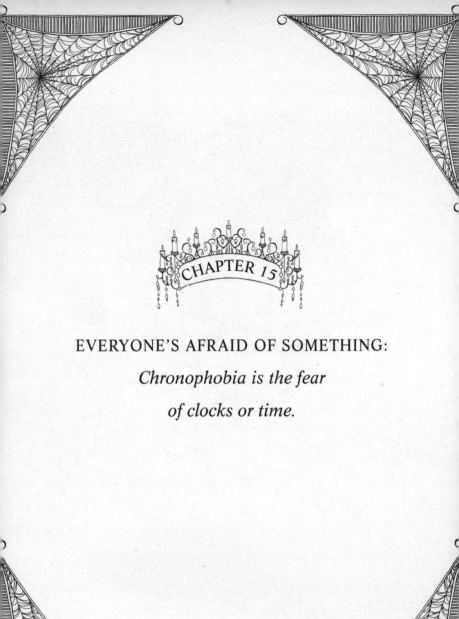

CHAPTER 15

EVERYONE'S AFRAID OF SOMETHING:

Chronophobia is the fear

of clocks or time.

The air had grown stale and thick in the office since Officer Patty had finished her inquisition. Hyacinth had dozed off with Celery neatly tucked away in her shirt. Next to her, Lulu played with her hair in between shooting hostile looks at Officer Patty. While at first irritated by Lulu's harsh stares, Officer Patty soon found solace in a decadent chocolate bar.

Watching Officer Patty slowly savor the candy bar was nearly more than Theo could handle. The young boy was in absolute agony as he debated whether or not to give in to his intense sugar cravings. A full tray of sweets and chocolates was mere inches away, taunting him mercilessly. Theo had never been one for self-control where candy was concerned, which made this all the more painful. If only Lulu and the others would look away for ten, maybe twenty seconds. That was all the time he needed to swallow a chocolate bar whole. Theo was more than willing to forgo chewing.

As Theo's hand moved slowly toward the tray of goodies, Lulu cocked her head in his direction. With a steely glare she shook her head meaningfully. It was clear: accepting the sweets was akin to betrayal. Theo thought Lulu was taking her loyalty a bit far, but what choice did he have?

Theo's sweet tooth silently raged as Garrison paced back and forth in front of the one-way mirror. He wasn't sure if anyone was even behind it, but the mere possibility of it irked him. This wasn't some sort of reality show where children paraded their fears on camera, Garrison thought while running his fingers through his messy blond locks.

For once Madeleine was utterly uninterested in Garrison. Her entire focus belonged to the cracked clock on the wall. The speed with which the second hand moved absolutely astounded Madeleine. Never did a second seem quite so fast. Was time always passing *this fast?* Channeling her inner Theo, Madeleine looked down at her hands, half expecting to see liver spots and wrinkles. Oh, dear, the young girl thought, jail was really getting to her.

Just as Madeleine prepared to ask for a glass of water and perhaps a doctor, the heavy metal door creaked open. The small gust of cool air was a welcome relief to the room's occupants. An older, white-haired officer with a stomach almost as big as Schmidty's waltzed in slowly.

"Patty, you can take off. We're releasing the kids back to the old people."

"Old*er* people," Mrs. Wellington corrected the man from down the hall. "Just because we're older than these prepubescent mutts does not mean we are *old*. Why, we're barely middle-aged . . . or at least I am . . ."

"Pipe down, tutu," the white-haired officer responded before turning back to Officer Patty. "So, like I was saying, we're letting the crazy lady leave with the kids."

"It's your call," Officer Patty said with a mouthful of chocolate.

"Actually, Patty, this was the governor's call," the white-haired officer explained before departing.

Madeleine, Lulu, Theo, and Garrison exchanged looks on hearing mention of the governor. Perhaps Mrs. Wellington was better connected than they thought. Theo felt both reassured and frightened by this information. While it was nice that Mrs. Wellington knew such a powerful man, it also reinforced just how little he knew about his tutu-wearing teacher.

"I suppose we ought to wake Hyacinth before we leave," Madeleine said unconvincingly.

"Yeah, I guess so," Lulu reluctantly agreed, knocking Hyacinth lightly across the head.

"Don't leave me!" Hyacinth yelped before she even opened her eyes, clearly afraid of being left behind.

"Honestly, Lulu, that's the only way you could think to wake her?" Theo asked disdainfully. "A fist bump to the head?"

"It was a *tap,* and if it was so important to you to wake Hyacinth with a serenade or with a handful of rose petals, then you should have stepped in."

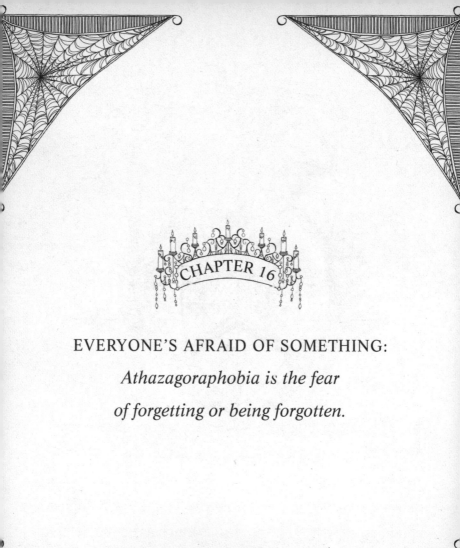

CHAPTER 16

EVERYONE'S AFRAID OF SOMETHING:

Athazagoraphobia is the fear

of forgetting or being forgotten.

Upon returning to the van, the group made a terribly distressing discovery. In the haste of their arrest, they had not only left their windows open, but they had all forgotten Macaroni. Thankfully, English bulldogs enjoy sleeping almost as much as eating, which was exactly how Macaroni passed the time.

Once seat belts were securely fastened, Mrs. Wellington arranged the mirrors so that she could see herself at all times. After a quick application of lipstick, she turned the key and began revving the engine. This act set off Theo's safety radar, prompting him to clear his throat loudly. "I think we've all learned an important lesson today about the dangers of speeding, reckless driving, and incarceration."

With a look of determination, Mrs. Wellington slammed her foot on the gas and stormed into traffic.

"Did you learn nothing, woman? Was jail one big joke to you?" Theo hollered as drivers honked and offered obscene hand gestures.

"Does anyone see a park? Trees? Greenery? Picnic tables? Maybe a swing set or sandbox?" Mrs. Wellington babbled manically as she drove erratically down the highway.

"Madame, not that I wish to increase your anxiety or the speed of this vehicle, but we only have fifteen minutes until the pageant starts. Maybe it's time to come up with a plan B," Schmidty said as he closed his eyes, unwilling to watch as Mrs. Wellington entered the city limits of Boston.

"I am morally opposed to plan B's and you know that, old man. They are the delinquents of the plan world, and I will have absolutely nothing to do with them."

"Yet another reason to always carry a cell phone. You never know when your mentally unhinged teacher dressed in a tutu is going to get lost on her way to a beauty pageant to meet her blackmailer," Theo explained earnestly to Hyacinth.

After a few nods of her head, Hyacinth smiled sweetly at Theo. "Thee Thee, Celery thinks you may have forgotten to brush your teeth this morning. I haven't noticed your halitosis, but that's what Celery's telling me. And she should know, since ferrets are known for their strong sense of smell."

"Well," Theo said with embarrassment as he covered his mouth and attempted to smell his own breath, "first of all, ferrets are known for nothing. They are the least distinguished members of the animal race. And second of all, it's not as if Celery smells so good herself. She doesn't shower, use toilet paper, or even own a toothbrush. And I've seen her pee on her own foot more than once."

"Is that the park?"

"No, Madame," Schmidty responded. "That is a single tree. I believe more than one tree is needed to qualify as a park."

"Why are there so many buildings and cars everywhere? It's as if they are hiding this park from me on purpose. This whole thing stinks of crown jealousy!"

Theo watched as Mrs. Wellington looked everywhere but at the road ahead. After taking a deep breath, he raised his hand and cleared his throat for the umpteenth time that day. "I don't mean to interrupt, Mrs. Wellington. Actually, on second thought, I do mean to interrupt you from NOT looking at the road," Theo said gravely. "I'm pretty sure the rule is six seconds, and I clocked you at seven. A lot could happen in seven seconds. I doubt you even realize how long seven seconds is. Let me demonstrate... one, two, three, four, five, six, seven... that didn't feel that long. Maybe I said them too quickly. One Mississippi, two—"

"Enough, Chubby! We haven't time for safety lessons."

"Excuse me, Madame, but I'm rather certain that sign says Franklin Park, or is that Fooman Pork?" Schmidty said, squinting severely. "So it's either the park or Chinese food."

Franklin Park, named for one of America's founding fathers, Benjamin Franklin, was an odd location to choose for the pageant. Not simply because it was Boston's largest park at 527 acres and therefore rather difficult to navigate, but also because it was outdoors. Pageants are generally conducted within a building, with electricity for hair dryers, curlers, and countless other appliances. As Mrs. Wellington parked the van illegally, she couldn't help but wonder what self-respecting beauty queen would arrange such an event in a park. It was simply blasphemous!

Without a second to spare, Mrs. Wellington charged into the park, sashaying past the pond, across the golf course, and finally under an archway. Once through the arch, she caught a whiff of hair spray and false-eyelash glue. Much like a bassett hound on the trail of a rabbit, she kept her nose pointed toward the ground as she drew long ragged breaths, digesting the many smells before continuing on her way. Normally such behavior would elicit a response from the group, but not today.

Mrs. Wellington's companions had long since stopped talking. The trek across the park had left them all winded, as well as dubious of the entire mission. Theo worried that this was a sophisticated setup so the burglar could hold them up and steal their wallets in the middle of the park. Schmidty now fretted that this was a ruse to get them away from Summerstone so the entire mansion could be rummaged for valuables, or worse, documented for a press release. The mere idea of it turned his stomach inside out.

As for Madeleine, she simply did not have the mental space to worry about others when she was in the middle of a park at the height of summer. This was spider season, and she was not about to allow another one to crawl across her ivory skin. Much as one would expect from a person suffering from post-traumatic stress disorder, Madeleine was experiencing horrid flashbacks. At least twice an hour her mind would momentarily go blank before being flooded by the memory of the spider hanging precariously over her face, then being brutally squished on her forehead. As she recalled this incident, an earthquake of emotions left her mute with nausea. The young lady simply could not speak a word while going through the torturous memories of the spider invasion. With all this racing through her mind, Madeleine did her best to stay with the group, but it wasn't easy. For on top of that, Madeleine insisted on flailing her arms about to keep any creepy-crawly creatures at bay.

As for Theo and Garrison, both were concentrating on extricating their hands from Hyacinth, who had rather amazingly managed to attach herself to *both* boys. This was Hyacinth's favorite type of walking; she was literally encumbered by people. Garrison and Theo did not share her enthusiasm for the hand-holding and could think of nothing but how clammy and repulsive their hands felt. Ahead of the boys, Lulu was hot on Mrs. Wellington's trail, anxious to confront the burglar who had caused everyone so much stress.

As for Macaroni, he was taken in by the lush scenery of the park, with its piles of moss-covered stones, winding paths, and endless trees. It had been quite some time since the chubby bulldog had ventured out of his normal territory, and he was thoroughly delighted by it. More than the new sights and sounds, it was the new smells that left him enchanted. Other than eating and sleeping, smelling was one of Macaroni's favorite leisure activities.

"That must be it!" Mrs. Wellington shouted as she pointed toward a red-and-white-striped tent at the edge of a cluster of trees.

"Madame, I believe that is a circus tent," Schmidty said.

The tent was at least two stories high, with multiple pointed peaks. It was impossible to see how far back the tent stretched, but it certainly didn't appear modest in size.

"This makes perfect sense. They couldn't possibly have a pageant outdoors. Everyone knows pageant makeup is not meant to be viewed in broad daylight."

"Yes, on that we most certainly agree," Schmidty said. "Speaking of which, would you care for a touch-up before entering the tent, Madame?"

"Dear man. Of course I would like a full reapplication of all makeup. This is the big comeback I have been waiting for. That burglar just may turn out to be the best thing that ever happened to me."

"Let's not get ahead of ourselves, Madame; it's been quite some time since your last real pageant. The ones we held in the ballroom with you and the cats don't count."

"Oh, don't be such a ninny! I'm a born winner. The spotlight has always loved me."

And with that, the students stared as a nearly blind

old man reapplied thick layers of pink eye shadow that perfectly coordinated with Mrs. Wellington's fluffy tutu. While clearly weak in the vision department, Schmidty was extremely quick. Why, he reapplied the makeup in under five minutes. Of course, speed and precision have very little to do with each other.

As Mrs. Wellington and company approached the tent, many crazy noises and scents took them by surprise. Not only was there the requisite odor of eyelash glue and hair spray in the air, there was also a rather pungent eucalyptus smell. As for the sounds, there were bells ringing and whistles blowing. It was all very much as one would expect at an actual circus.

Theo took a few deep breaths before shaking his head in disappointment. "I was kind of expecting perfume and baby powder, not... what is that?"

"The smell of denture cream and hearing aids," Lulu remarked drily. "These are Mrs. Wellington's peers, after all."

"This is probably going to scar me," Garrison muttered to Madeleine. "I may never be able to look at my grandma the same way again."

"Highly probable," Madeleine agreed, while continuing to flail her arms about. "I don't mean to be pushy, Mrs. Wellington, as I know you haven't been part of a pageant in ages, but I am more than ready to get out of the great outdoors and away from its many creepy-crawly creatures. I'm rather certain I can hear insect wings flapping and spiders' pads sticking right this second..."

Mrs. Wellington completely ignored Madeleine while once again straightening out her tutu and running her hands over her wig.

"Contestants, before we enter, I must, as your teacher, prepare you for the wide range of emotions you will be confronted with. Some of you may feel jealous or envious while watching me in my full glory, with the crowd cheering loudly, perhaps even chanting my name. Please make mental notes of said experience, since I would love to hear about it on the car ride home as well as every day for the rest of my life. Others may go into absolute shock, stunned by the sight of so many gorgeous women in one place. No need to make mental notes about anyone else's beauty, though." Mrs. Wellington smiled largely while pulling back the tent's flap.

The group was greeted by a scrawny woman with

long noodlelike arms. Rather surprisingly, she was dressed in a red top hat, thick black veil, corseted dress, and a belt of bells. It certainly wasn't the traditional pink dress with rhinestones they were expecting from a pageant woman.

"Welcome. I'm Finca, the master of ceremonies," the top-hat woman said in a gravelly voice. "Is this your first time?"

"I won't even dignify that with a response."

"Very well," Finca said as she walked, bells jingling, toward another tent flap.

She pulled back the thick red-and-white plastic drape and motioned for the group to enter. Mrs. Wellington placed her right hand on her hip and led Schmidty, Macaroni, and the children into the tent.

The instant they entered, they stopped, mouths agape. This was not what they were expecting.

CHAPTER 17

EVERYONE'S AFRAID OF SOMETHING:

Wiccaphobia is the fear

of witches or witchcraft.

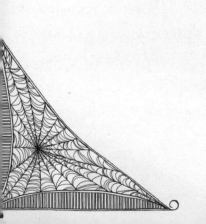
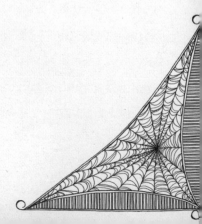

The tent bustled with people and animals pushing to and fro as the students remained paralyzed in shock. The sound of bells, whistles, and barking filled the densely crowded space. But most notably, the people were dressed as dogs and the dogs dressed as people. Grown men and women walked around with face paint, furry ears, and plastic snouts while their dogs wore lipstick, wigs, and a variety of outfits.

"It's a beauty pageant for dogs!" Mrs. Wellington

expounded enthusiastically as she pointed to a sparkly sign that read THE PAGEANT OF POOCHES!

"Madame, you look a tad manic. Is everything all right?"

"Old man, this is it! This is where I belong. These are *my people,*" Mrs. Wellington said as she surveyed her surroundings.

Awash in euphoria, Mrs. Wellington literally skipped into the adjoining room, which housed a large circular stage. French bulldogs costumed in tall white wigs and corseted dresses proudly pranced around the stage. This was the height of French fashion circa the late 1700s, only worn by dogs.

Schmidty, Macaroni, and the children crowded around Mrs. Wellington in an attempt to get the old woman's attention.

"Excuse me," Madeleine said firmly as she tapped on Mrs. Wellington's arm. "We must stay focused! Mrs. Wellington, the fate of the school depends on your finding this burglar."

"But there are dogs in wigs," Mrs. Wellington mumbled as if under a spell.

"That doesn't matter! We need to find this burglar.

Don't you realize that if you lose the school, we lose any chance of getting better?" Madeleine pleaded. "Look at me! I am wearing a shower cap in public! Clearly, there is much work to be done!"

"Dogs...wigs...dresses...earrings...lipstick..." Mrs. Wellington uttered inarticulately, all the while never taking her eyes off the stage.

"Maddie's right," Garrison said. "Whoever is behind this has the power to ruin the school and us. I don't want to spend my life as a pretend surfer. I don't want my whole identity to be based on a lie, you know?"

"I know how you feel; I'm getting pretty tired of all the fake trips to the bathroom when I go out with my family," Lulu admitted. "School of Fear is the only thing that's ever helped me. Hypnosis, therapy, bribery... nothing else has worked."

"I hate to admit it, but it's only a matter of time before my brothers and sisters catch me spying on them...and then they'll pelt me with pickled eggs from the Korean deli...and I don't even like eggs...and frankly, I'm more than a little tired of worrying about them twenty-four–seven. If this keeps up I'll need Botox by high school," Theo said dramatically as he shook his head.

"Celery says this is better than *Oprah*. Besties having emotional breakthroughs! It's bonding at its finest," Hyacinth said proudly.

"And now it's been ruined," Lulu snapped at her.

"With Mrs. Wellington in her current state," Madeleine said as she looked at the elderly woman pushing through the crowd with Macaroni on her shoulders, "finding the burglar falls to us. We must move quickly and efficiently, so I suggest we break up into groups and do our best to find this burglar. Seeing as this person has intimate knowledge of the school, I wouldn't be surprised if they found us. Plus, we are rather conspicuous, being the only people not dressed as canines."

"I'll go with Maddie, since Theo and Garrison seem rather attached to Hyacinth," Lulu said with a smirk.

"Oh my gosh! Celery and I are going on a double friend date with Theo and Garrison!"

"Celery better not be *my* date," Theo huffed. "This isn't the first time someone has tried to set me up with a ferret."

"Schmidty, are you all right on your own?"

"Of course, Miss Madeleine," Schmidty said honestly.

"Working for Madame has prepared me to handle almost anything pageant-related."

Ahead of the group was a literal maze of rooms. Unsure where to start, Garrison decided to go with the closest. The young boy pulled on Hyacinth, who in turn pulled on Theo, and with that the train of kids and one ferret was off. Past barrels, hay bushels, and under a twinkling arch the three did go, never once looking back to see which direction their friends had gone.

The next room was vastly more crowded, causing enormous navigational problems for the three. While Garrison, Hyacinth, and Theo were pushed and batted by humans and dogs alike, the audience erupted in a chorus of oohs and ahhs.

"I can't see the stage. What's happening?" Garrison asked Hyacinth and Theo.

"My guess is a dog making a sandwich, or maybe some sort of pasta dish. Yes, a dog cooking show! Why hasn't someone thought of this before? It's genius!"

"Celery doesn't think that is even remotely possible. Actually, Celery never agrees with anything you say, Theo."

"Well, isn't that charming—a judgmental ferret,"

Theo said gruffly as the crowd erupted in a storm of clapping.

"For all we know, Mrs. Wellington is up there applying makeup to Macaroni," Garrison said as he scanned the crowd for anyone suspicious. This was no simple feat; after all, the crowd did consist of eccentrics dressed as canines.

"Celery thinks that sounds more likely than the dog cooking show," Hyacinth said smugly.

Theo gave Celery a distasteful look. He was fed up with the rodent's insults. After all, he hadn't even mentioned that the ferret had crooked yellow teeth and a nail situation almost as questionable as Schmidty's.

Garrison led the threesome to the edge of the room, where they pushed and prodded their way along the tent's walls. After more than a few bumps and bruises, they were able to catch a glimpse of the stage. A nimble-footed golden retriever pranced from side to side, tossing a long white bone in the air, only to catch it seconds later. The dog was costumed in a small red-and-gold cap that reminded Theo of a bellhop's, with red bands around each paw. It really was rather spectacular how much the dog could accomplish while the bone was up in the air, and then manage to catch it. There was simply no denying it; this dog was exceptionally talented. He could roll over, walk on his hind legs, and leap like a ballerina, all before catching the bone from a seated position.

For a moment Theo, Hyacinth, and Garrison were entirely absorbed by the show and completely forgot the task at hand. It wasn't until Finca appeared that they were reminded of their purpose. The woman's belt of bells jangled as she shuffled across the stage, her octopus arms dangling by her side.

"Barclay the Bone Baton Boy," Finca said in a raspy voice. "A talented dog if I do say so myself. And now for the next contestant—Pierre the Pug!"

"OK, we need to keep moving," Garrison whispered. "We have a lot of ground to cover."

"Fine," Theo lamented, "although I am a little curious about this pug."

With a quick shake of the head, Garrison continued leading Hyacinth and Theo through the crowd, often getting pushed and kicked along the way. Just as the threesome neared the perimeter of the large mass of people, Pierre released a high-pitched howl that frightened

Celery. The small ferret's gray fur stood on end as her beady little eyes raced around the room. Clearly in an extreme state of panic, the ferret leapt from Hyacinth's shoulder and instantly disappeared into the swarm of people.

"Celery!" Hyacinth screamed, causing a murmur to run through the crowd. "Don't leave me! You're my number one bestie! Please!"

On her hands and knees, the petite girl dove after Celery. As Hyacinth crawled at warp speed, calling the ferret's name incessantly, people attempted to hush her for Pierre's sake, but she simply couldn't be stopped. By now Theo and Garrison had completely lost sight of the girl in the dense crowd and could hear her voice only faintly over the cheers and hollers of the pageant. Both boys massaged their hands as they looked at each other, unsure what to do next.

In a nearby room Madeleine and Lulu moved stealthily through the crowd, scanning each person carefully. If it hadn't been such a serious situation, Lulu would have quite enjoyed playing detective for the afternoon. After all, she had always fancied the notion of a career in the intelligence field.

"I simply don't understand why the people are dressed as dogs," Madeleine whispered to Lulu as the two scoured the room with their eyes. "The pageant is for the dogs, not the people."

"They're probably humiliated that this is their idea of a good time. Think about it. What kinds of people enjoy dressing their dogs in formal wear?"

"Formal wear?" Madeleine asked, prompting Lulu to nod her head toward the back of the tent. On a small stage in the corner, under a red-lettered banner proclaiming DACHSHUND DIVAS, were three dogs in wigs, lipstick, and multiple pearl necklaces.

"You know the sick thing? I bet those are real pearls," Lulu said as she continued through the room.

Poor Schmidty really shouldn't have been left on his own, as his vision in the faint lighting was quite diminished. It had taken him an entire ten minutes to realize that the man looking at him was actually his own shadow.

Following the shadow incident, Schmidty headed

into the next room, bumping into quite a few men, women, and dogs along the way. He had never been very fond of crowds, but the current situation made him even more nervous. The scene was far too chaotic for the burglar to be able to find them. In addition, Schmidty worried about what sort of burglar would choose such a location for a meeting. He had watched enough films to know that this should have taken place in a deserted parking garage or a dark alley.

Oh, the whole thing was simply ludicrous, Schmidty thought as he shimmied toward a stage filled with miniature pinschers. Schmidty had never been fond of min pins, as they are known. Their bossy nature reminded him far too much of Mrs. Wellington.

As the min pins' martial marching came to a close, Finca stepped onto the stage and began assessing each of the dogs. The strange woman's spindly arms were so long that she could pet the dogs from a standing position.

"Based on form, fierceness, and fur, I declare Charles the winner," Finca proclaimed hoarsely. "And remember, in a few short minutes, Bulldog Ballerinas will begin in the main tent."

If ever a lightbulb were to appear above Schmidty's head, it would most certainly have happened now. If this burglar knew as much about Madame as Schmidty believed, there would be no better place to find him.

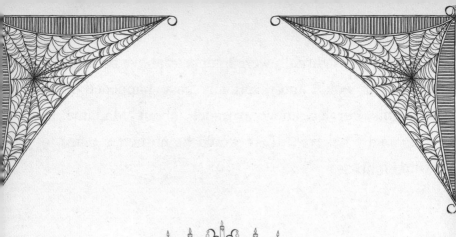

CHAPTER 18

EVERYONE'S AFRAID OF SOMETHING:

Xanthophobia is the fear

of the color yellow.

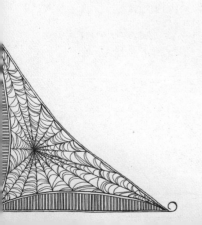
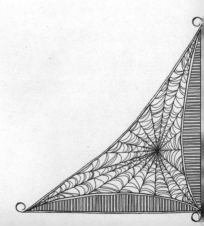

Theo and Garrison had stood still without uttering a word for over three minutes. On the edge of a bustling crowd of people and dogs, the two boys looked at each other, unsure what to do next.

"Hyacinth didn't want us to follow her, did she?" Garrison asked, pretending not to know the unbelievably obvious answer to his question.

"I doubt it," Theo played along. "I actually think Celery wanted some alone time with Hyacinth and that's why she ran off. It would have been rude if we had gone after them, kind of like crashing a date."

"Totally. Plus, she wouldn't want us to forget about Mrs. Wellington and the burglar. I mean, someone needs to stay on track, right?"

"Right," Theo agreed as he continued to massage his hand. "Now, what do you think the likelihood is of finding a snack cart or food court in here?"

"Theo, has anyone ever checked to make sure you don't have a worm in your stomach?"

"Tons of times," Theo responded casually. "I'd say a minimum of twice a year."

Garrison trailed Theo into the next room, all the while wondering if it were possible for this chubby boy ever to feel full. Fortunately, Lulu and Madeleine entered the main tent at the same time the boys did. As the girls were the only other noncostumed people, they were rather easy to spot.

"Where's Hyacinth?" Lulu blurted out as the boys approached.

"Um, she and Celery wanted some alone time to catch up, or something like that. You know ferrets; they are so secretive," Theo explained.

"Yeah, right," Lulu said with a laugh. "I've got to hand it to you, Theo. I didn't think you had it in you to ditch the little bugger."

"There was no ditching, Lulu. Don't try to besmirch my good name!"

"That sounds like a line you stole from a movie."

"That doesn't make it any less true."

"All right, enough," Madeleine said firmly. "Did either of you see anything suspicious? Or perhaps Mrs. Wellington and Macaroni?"

"Nope," Garrison responded.

"I think the burglar will most likely approach only Mrs. Wellington, so we ought to locate her, then keep a very keen eye on her."

"I don't think that's going to be a problem," Lulu said as she pointed to the main stage, where Finca stood beneath a BALLERINA BULLDOGS sign.

"Hello, everyone. As most of you already know, I am Finca, master of ceremonies, and it is my great honor to announce Ballerina Bulldogs, my favorite event of the night."

As the woman spoke, Madeleine spotted Schmidty across the stage, squinting at the crowd. While the old man could clearly not see them, Madeleine was grateful to have located at least one of the missing members of the party.

"This is just wrong—those dogs are humiliated," Garrison said as owners led their tutu-clad English bulldogs onstage.

"What kind of name is Finca?" Theo asked no one in particular. "It has a real star quality to it, kind of like Cher or Madonna. I could definitely see myself naming my daughter that."

"You are worse than Hyacinth, talking about your kids. Um, wake-up call? You haven't even hit puberty," Lulu said, rolling her eyes.

"Well, you don't have to rub it in. And why are you mentioning Hyacinth? Just to torment me? The guilt is suffocating me!"

"Look! There she is," Madeleine whispered to the others. "In the name of the Queen, what has Mrs. Wellington done to herself?"

"Wow, that is intense," Garrison said, averting his eyes in embarrassment.

"It's just not pretty," Lulu stated honestly.

"For either of them," Theo said, shaking his head.

"We must stay vigilant about scanning the crowd," Madeleine instructed the others. "The burglar is probably watching Mrs. Wellington just like we are . . . although there is a chance he doesn't recognize her in light of the current . . . situation."

Even in the dim candlelight, Mrs. Wellington's fashion eccentricity was wholly visible. Half of her tutu had been ripped off and fastened onto Macaroni as a skirt. In addition, Mrs. Wellington had given the bulldog her brown bob wig to wear and had placed Macaroni's collar around her own head like a sweatband. But perhaps most ghastly were the large gobs of Vaseline falling out of both their mouths. Mrs. Wellington believed that a beauty queen should coat his or her teeth with Vaseline for a shiny smile.

While the other English bulldogs onstage were dressed in tutus and tights, none of them were wearing a wig. And though Mrs. Wellington was the only owner onstage without a dog costume on, she still managed to look the craziest by at least a mile. Judging by her behavior, one couldn't quite be sure if Mrs. Wellington knew that this was a dog pageant.

Across the stage, Schmidty's cheeks blushed bright

red. The elderly man was terribly concerned about what such an outfit could do to Macaroni's self-esteem and sense of masculinity. Sure, Macaroni wore pajamas and enjoyed the odd pedicure, but this was too much. Schmidty patted his comb-over nervously as he looked for the stairs to the stage. Something simply had to be done.

"I think Schmidty's going to try to lure Mrs. Wellington down," Theo whispered to the others. But before Schmidty was able to locate the stairs, a couple in matching yellow sweaters, droopy brown ears, and black snouts waltzed onto the stage. As the couple approached Finca, it became clear that the woman was carrying a poodle in a baby carrier on her chest.

"Finca, we are sorry to interrupt," the man said in a chipper tone, "but this is a dog emergency. A dog's life is literally hanging in the balance here tonight."

"It better be, since you interrupted my most important show of the night." Finca grunted angrily at the couple, who she hoped would not try to pass their poodle off as a bulldog.

"Please, you have to believe us. That poor bulldog over there in the wig is in terrible trouble!" the woman with the poodle shrieked, "and that old woman in half a tutu, Mrs. Wellington, is to blame!"

"Excuse me?" Mrs. Wellington said, suddenly snapping to attention. "You are ruining our moment. Could we not discuss this after Macaroni and I win? Perhaps over tea and trophies?"

"No, we most certainly cannot postpone this conversation. Macaroni is being mistreated, and we expect you to answer for it in front of your dog-loving peers," the man said tensely from under his large black snout.

"So *you're* the sticky-fingered twits who broke into Summerstone and stole all my wigs!" Mrs. Wellington responded, shaking her head judgmentally at the couple.

"No, we're the Knapps," they chimed in unison before removing their ears and snouts.

"Have you any idea what life is like for a beauty queen with only one wig? It's absolute torture!" claimed Mrs. Wellington.

"Torture is what you are doing to that dog," Mr. Knapp announced confidently, "and we are here to stop you."

"What?" Mrs. Wellington asked in genuine confusion. "You mean the wig and tutu?"

"No. We actually think dogs enjoy dressing up," Mrs. Knapp responded. "It helps get them in touch with their creativity."

"Well, at least we agree on that."

"OK, so it's not the tutu," Finca interjected. "Let's get on with this; we've got a pageant happening here."

"Mrs. Wellington does not have a doggy seat belt for Macaroni!" Mr. Knapp blurted out.

"Would you allow your babies to ride without a seat belt?" Mrs. Knapp dramatically asked the crowd. "Any sudden braking, and boom—baby through the windshield!"

"It's true that I do not have a seat belt for Macaroni," Mrs. Wellington admitted to the Knapps, Finca, and the crowd, "but that is only because I don't have a car, you nitwits!"

"On top of that, you refuse to get him braces or acupuncture, and you haven't even enrolled him in yoga! Dogs need yoga to unwind!" Mrs. Knapp screeched, her emotion apparent.

"Yoga? Macaroni doesn't even like to stretch, let alone do yoga. He is a bulldog, and everyone knows they lack the mental and physical capacity for yoga. As dog people, I thought you would have known that, but clearly I was wrong. Then again, what can I expect from wig thieves!"

"What about the way you make him work? Polishing furniture with his tongue?" Mrs. Knapp continued fiercely.

"I would never make Macaroni do any such thing. I save all demeaning jobs for my manservant, Schmidty."

At that moment Schmidty attempted to pull himself onto the stage, but as he was rather thick and mountain-like at his waist, he couldn't quite manage it.

"Oh, there's Schmidty now! See him? The one with the comb-over and very large belly. You can ask him yourself!" Mrs. Wellington shot back victoriously. "He is most definitely the only one being mistreated in my care, and that is only because he enjoys it so much."

Finca, feeling sorry for the floundering Schmidty, used her long arms to aid the rotund man as he clambered onto the stage.

"Thank you so much, Miss Finca. I haven't been able to get to the gym lately," Schmidty mumbled with embarrassment as he stood up.

"It's true, Mr. and Mrs. Knapp, it is I, not Macaroni,

who on occasion has cleaned the furniture with my own saliva and tongue. I worked the hardest on Grace's shell, which you cruelly stole from Summerstone and from me. So before you continue with Madame, you must explain your dastardly theft to me."

"We were trying to rescue Macaroni," Mr. Knapp expounded in a discombobulated manner, "but Macaroni never left your side or Mrs. Wellington's side for a second, so we started taking random items to throw you off. We even bribed that unusual man in the forest to distract you. We will happily return all that stuff—we just want Macaroni!"

"Well, you can't have him," Schmidty said firmly.

"You don't deserve him!" Mrs. Knapp shot back.

"I most certainly do! I brush this dog's teeth twice a day!"

"Yes, you may brush his teeth, but what about the horrible and dangerous manner in which you feed him?" Mr. Knapp said while trying to maintain a smile.

"Of all the cockamamie nonsense I have heard in my life, this is the absolute worst," Mrs. Wellington chimed in. "The dog eats at the table, on a chair, from a sterling silver bowl, in the formal dining room at my mansion.

What could be more civilized than that? And don't say dressing him in a tuxedo, because we tried that, and he simply won't have it."

"How about placing each piece of kibble delicately on Macaroni's tongue to make sure he doesn't eat too quickly and choke?" Mrs. Knapp said tensely.

"Why stop there? Perhaps you should prechew the food for your dog too?" Mrs. Wellington shot back sarcastically.

"We tried that. Jeffrey didn't like it. His pet therapist said it made him feel too much like a bird," Mrs. Knapp responded, causing the crowd to gasp in disgust.

"Stop!" Finca screamed. "As master of ceremonies, I am putting an end to this insanity!"

"Thank you," Mr. and Mrs. Knapp said in unison. "This is exactly why we came here. We knew you would understand."

"Understand?" Finca said before maniacally laughing. "The only thing I understand is that you have ruined my favorite part of the Pooch Pageant, and for that you will pay."

"What?" Mr. and Mrs. Knapp gasped, in shock.

"I am blacklisting you from every specialty pet store

in the Northeast region. That means no doggy sweaters, no doggy shoes, no doggy massages, and definitely no doggy yoga. You'll be lucky if Petco lets you in the door."

Mrs. Knapp immediately collapsed into hysterics, forcing her husband to carry her and Jeffrey offstage.

"Well done, Finca," Mrs. Wellington said victoriously. "Well done."

"Oh, I'm not done, Wellington," Finca responded devilishly.

"Oh dear. I doubt those two can take any more," Mrs. Wellington said truthfully.

"Are you enjoying the pageant, Mrs. Wellington?"

"This is the happiest day of my life! I never knew that two of my great passions, pageantry and dogs, could be combined. It's the most marvelous, spectacular place on earth!"

"It is, isn't it?" Finca said as she stared Mrs. Wellington straight in the eye. "Unfortunately, this is the first and only time you will ever be allowed in a pooch pageant. For your act of disorderly conduct I am banishing you from all pooch pageants worldwide for the remainder of your life!"

"No!" Mrs. Wellington wailed as she dropped to her knees. "Please, I will do anything! Don't take this away from me! From us! What has Macaroni done to deserve this?"

"I am afraid the damage is done," Finca said unemotionally.

"Mrs. Wellington," Hyacinth screamed as she hoisted herself onto the stage with Celery on her shoulder, "where are those rotten boys? Celery wants to punish them!"

"All of you, out!!!!!!!!!!!" Finca roared angrily. "Out! Out this second, or I'll ban you from buying canine clothes!"

CHAPTER 19

EVERYONE'S AFRAID OF SOMETHING:

Atychiphobia is the fear

of failure.

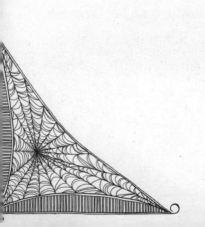
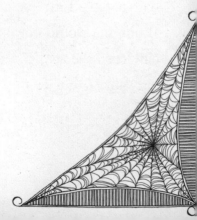

F ranklin Park was aglow with the last remnants of
the day's sun when Mrs. Wellington stepped deject-
edly out of the red-and-white-striped tent. The soft
breeze on her scalp reminded the old woman dressed in
half a pink tutu that Macaroni still had her wig on.
While she would never admit it to Schmidty or even the
children, she was a tad disappointed that the Knapps
had turned out to be the burglars. It was a great deal

more soothing to her ego to believe that a former rival still feared her beauty.

Ever the attentive manservant, Schmidty placed the wig back on Mrs. Wellington's head after removing Macaroni's collar. He then moved on to Macaroni, removing the tutu. Schmidty simply could not bear to see the dog dressed in pink tulle for one more second.

Mrs. Wellington and Schmidty led the pack back to the van, keeping a fairly brisk pace considering their advanced years. A few steps behind Mrs. Wellington and Schmidty, Lulu, Garrison, and Madeleine walked in silence. Madeleine's arms were flailing about as usual in a lame effort to dissuade bugs or insects from approaching. "Would it be a terrible bother to ask you both to wave your arms around as well? If there are six arms instead of two, I have a higher chance of surviving the walk to the van without a run-in."

"Sure," Garrison agreed, too tired to put up a fuss over Madeleine's irrational request.

"Great. In addition to walking behind an old woman in half a tutu and a man with pants pulled up to his neck, the three of us are waving our arms around like a bunch of wackos," Lulu grumbled. "No wonder we got kicked out of a dog pageant for being too weird."

Quite a way behind the arm-wavers were Theo, Hyacinth, and Macaroni. Theo was exhausted from all the pageantry hoopla and moving at an exceptionally slow pace.

"Thee Thee, snap to it! Celery thinks you need to pick up the pace big-time!"

"I haven't had a bite of food in hours. Do you have any idea what that does to a growing man?"

Hyacinth attempted to pull Theo along, but the boy refused to increase his speed. Macaroni then passed Hyacinth and Theo, much to the girl's aggravation. The fact that a bulldog could waddle faster than Theo seemed an insult to the natural order. Normally, Hyacinth wouldn't have cared in the slightest, but she was still more than a bit peeved about having been abandoned in the tent.

"Stop pulling my arm. I have very sensitive joints," Theo protested.

"Celery would like to know if a doctor gave you that diagnosis."

"Kind of...I diagnosed myself after watching an actor pretending to be a doctor on television."

"Celery says that there is nothing wrong with your arm. She says the only problem you have is that you're out of shape! Big-time!"

"Tell your ferret that I don't do very well with negative reinforcement. If you really want to help the situation, you could sing something from *High School Musical* to get my enthusiasm back up."

"Hyacinth," Lulu hollered back from up ahead.

"Hyhy," Hyacinth corrected.

"Really? You're still correcting us," Lulu said as she stopped and turned to look at Hyacinth. "Clearly that nickname isn't sticking; I think it's time to let it go. Oh, and if you start singing, I can't be held responsible for what I'll do."

"Lulu, you shouldn't threaten her—she is only a child. A highly bothersome one, but a child nonetheless," Madeleine added in a rather stern voice.

"Thank you, Mad Mad!" Hyacinth said, with a little too much enthusiasm.

"Oh, enough with the Mad Mad! It's time you plainly accept that you are not very good at coming up with nicknames, Hyacinth. In truth, neither am I. That's why I simply call everyone by their proper name."

"Celery thinks you secretly like being called Mad Mad and that I should keep doing it no matter what you say!"

"Tell Celery that in some parts of England, people eat ferrets," Madeleine said harshly.

Tired, irritated, and hungry, the students walked the remainder of the way back to the van in silence. Other than Macaroni's heavy panting and the grasshoppers chirping, there was nary a sound to be heard.

Without a pageant start time to make, everyone expected Mrs. Wellington to obey basic traffic laws, look at the road, and generally make an effort to get them home alive. However, as soon as the old woman turned the key, she stomped on the gas pedal and took her eyes off the road.

"Madame, as pleasurable as almost dying and being arrested was on the drive here, we are not in any rush to get home, so perhaps you could slow to within ten miles of the speed limit," Schmidty said as the van's tires squealed loudly while rounding a corner.

"Yes, I suppose that is true. It's not as if anyone is waiting for us at home."

"Actually, the cats are home, but they're definitely not waiting for us, since they probably haven't noticed we're gone because they sleep all day," Theo expounded, shaking his head. "Talk about lazy."

"Excuse me, but have you all forgotten that there are hundreds of spiders and beetles roaming the house, just waiting for us to get home? Oh, no! Simply thinking about it makes me ill," Madeleine wailed.

"Then stop thinking about it," Garrison said firmly, "because I really don't want you to get sick in the car. And I say this both as a friend and as the boy sitting next to you."

The students nodded in and out of consciousness, waking only for the sound of cars honking or tires screeching. By the time Mrs. Wellington turned onto Main Street, everyone was wide awake and salivating over the thought of a warm meal before bed.

Much to Mrs. Wellington's and Schmidty's surprise, the sheriff was standing outside the station. Even in the long shadow cast by the brim of the sheriff's hat, Schmidty could see that something was horribly wrong. The sheriff wasn't a man who blanched easily, but he was downright pale. Oblivious to the sheriff's expression, Mrs. Wellington exited the van while Schmidty remained seated to prepare himself for what was to come.

"Hello, Sheriff. How civilized of you to greet us at the curb," Mrs. Wellington said with a smile. "I am loath to disappoint you, but I did not come home with a trophy, nor did Macaroni, but only because those silly Knapps got us thrown out of the doggy pageant! Honestly, those two are such a nuisance, and their fashion sense is absolutely catastrophic. I think we ought to lobby Congress to pass a law about married couples dressing in matching outfits."

"Mrs. Wellington, I think you'd better come inside. I've got some troubling news to share with you, and I think you may need to be seated."

"Oh, no!" Mrs. Wellington gasped loudly, not moving an inch, "Don't tell me Schmidty has died!"

"What? No. He's right there," the sheriff said as Schmidty joined the two on the sidewalk, leaving Macaroni and the children in the van.

"Oh, thank heavens! For a second I thought you were dead," Mrs. Wellington said as she turned to Schmidty.

"Thought or hoped?" the old man spat back. "Sheriff,

I sense from your worried expression that something fairly dire has transpired. Might I suppose that Munchauser has stolen another racehorse? Or lost his cat in a poker game?"

"I wish I could say yes, but this isn't about Munchauser. It's about someone named Sylvie Montgomery."

"Sylvie who?" Mrs. Wellington asked, perplexed.

"I don't recall Madame ever having had a student named Sylvie."

"Sylvie isn't a former student. She's a reporter, and she arrived in town about an hour ago. Mrs. Wellington, she knows about the school. And from what she was describing to me, her interpretations of your methods are pretty horrible. I'm sure you both can imagine how awful things sound when taken out of context by someone who hasn't been to the school."

"But how," Schmidty whispered, "how could she know so much about us?"

"Apparently, someone gave her the inside scoop at the dog beauty pageant."

"Oh, dear," Schmidty mumbled.

"And that's not the worst of it," the sheriff continued.

"This woman is on the verge of exposing my school, a place I have raised as if it were my very own child, and yet there is something worse? How is that even possible? And don't say she killed Schmidty. I don't think I could handle it..."

"Again, Madame, I am right here, utterly alive."

"Oh, thank heavens," Mrs. Wellington said dramatically, her hand pressed to her forehead.

"Sylvie knows about Abernathy. Her angle is that your unorthodox tactics drove him to live in the woods, alone and cut off from society. It's pretty sensational stuff."

"How long do we have?" Mrs. Wellington muttered.

"Sylvie says she's going to run the story at the end of the month. She's only waiting so she can get front-page placement."

"I never thought it would end this way, but then again, I never thought it would end," Mrs. Wellington said, her face pale—with the exception of her generously applied eye shadow and lipstick. "I suppose we ought to prepare or mourn or do whatever it is that people do when something dies. Sheriff, would you drive us back to Summerstone now?"

During the ride back to the base of Summerstone the children sensed something was wrong, but they couldn't quite figure out what had happened. Theo watched Mrs. Wellington and Schmidty closely, noting the look of pure agony on both their faces. As bad as seeing Macaroni dressed in a tutu had been, Theo knew Schmidty could not possibly have such a tortured expression over something that silly. And as for Mrs. Wellington—sure, she had been banned from dog pageants, but she could always start her own. No, it was something else, Theo thought as the van stopped at the bottom of the mountain. The five students, Macaroni, Schmidty, and Mrs. Wellington rode the SVT in silence. It wasn't until the group got to Summerstone's imposing front door that someone finally said something.

"I'm sorry, but would everyone mind terribly if I waited out here while you tried to round up the spiders and beetles?" Madeleine asked. "And please keep your eyes peeled for any sort of crossbreeding between the two. I'm rather certain it's taken place."

"No one minds in the slightest," Mrs. Wellington said kindly, "although I will be retiring for the night, so you will be on your own. Schmidty, I trust that you can handle the situation after my departure."

"Of course, Madame."

"I suppose that's one good thing; you won't have to call me Madame anymore."

"Oh, no, I shall always call you Madame. Our relationship could not exist without a rigid hierarchy."

"So true, old man, so true," Mrs. Wellington said meekly before walking into Summerstone.

"Wow, she is really depressed about being kicked out of that pageant," Garrison said, shaking his head in shock. "I had no idea dogs in costume could mean so much to someone."

"I'm not so sure about that. Is that what's happening?" Lulu asked Schmidty pointedly, sensing there was more to the situation.

"No, I'm afraid it's nothing to do with that. Unfortunately, it appears that at the pageant a reporter was given inside information about our institution, including details of Mrs. Wellington's many techniques, and perhaps most damaging, everything about Abernathy. The article will be the end of us."

"Those stupid Knapps! I am going to kidnap Jeffrey just to punish them! They're going to regret they ever messed with us!" Lulu screeched.

"Yeah!" Theo yelled. "And we'll dress him up in really bad clothes too. He'll be laughed out of every dog park in Massachusetts."

"I'm sorry to inform you, but it wasn't the Knapps. According to the sheriff, the reporter was given the inside scoop by one of our students. And while the student is not mentioned by name since she is a minor, it does state that she traveled with a pet ferret."

Hyacinth immediately lowered her eyes to the ground in shame.

"Why, you despicable, evil, pestilent, virulent little maggot," Madeleine exploded furiously. "If I weren't terrified to go into the house, I'd storm away, because simply looking at you makes me ill!"

"What? No, Mad Mad! You can't be angry at me. We're besties. It wasn't my fault. Celery said it was OK to tell Sylvie, because she is a bestie too! Sylvie and Hyhy, friends forever! I never would have done it if Celery hadn't said it was OK. Please believe me. I'm innocent in all this. It's all Celery's fault!"

"Pathetic! You can't even own your own mistake; you're blaming it on a ferret," Lulu yelled at the small child in a pantsuit.

"No, Lulu, please understand. Sylvie is a bestie like you guys. I don't keep anything from my besties. I thought that's what besties did. I thought they held hands and told each other all their secrets."

"You know what is so sad about this whole thing?" Theo asked rhetorically. "It's that you are so obsessed with being friends with everyone, but you don't even know the first thing about friendship. You're not even a good friend to your ferret. You blame all your mean comments and mistakes on her. I know for a fact that if I had left Garrison, Madeleine, or Lulu alone with a reporter for days, they would never have betrayed anyone, least of all Mrs. Wellington."

"I said I was sorry," Hyacinth mumbled.

"I think it's best that you and Celery go to your room, Hyacinth. The rest of us have quite a lot of spider-catching to do before Madeleine can go to bed," Schmidty said unemotionally.

"I can help!"

"We don't want your help," Garrison said firmly. "We don't want anything to do with you."

CHAPTER 20

EVERYONE'S AFRAID OF SOMETHING:

Enissophobia is the fear

of criticism.

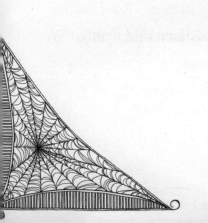
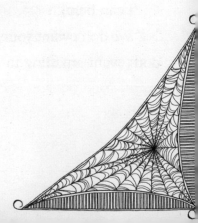

Hyacinth entered Summerstone's foyer with a stoic expression, her emotions seemingly contained. The young girl had barely reached the staircase when her legs began to tremble. Soon her chest tightened, and she felt as though she could barely breathe. Tears poured down her cheeks as she mounted the stairs reluctantly. With each step Hyacinth fought the overwhelming urge to run back outside and throw herself on the mercy of the others. She couldn't explain why, but her instincts had always told her to flee when left alone. It was this sense of panic that had driven her to always have a companion.

Hyacinth recognized that there was no rational reason to fear being alone; however, the experience left her filled with a sense of panic. Her mind raced as her emotions surged, leaving little to no room for logic. She started for the door, but stopped suddenly. Hyacinth knew they would force her to return, and she couldn't bear to walk those stairs alone again. Moreover, seeing her classmates' critical expressions would only augment her already overwhelming guilt and shame about the situation.

Alone in her bedroom, Hyacinth curled up next to Celery and cried. She had never felt quite so small and insignificant as she did on that bed. The world seemed a cold and lonely place, and the worst part was, she had made it that way. Oddly, after thoroughly soaking both her pillowcase and her ferret with tears, Hyacinth began to think clearly for the first time since arriving at School of Fear.

Hyacinth didn't really know that much about the others, and they knew next to nothing about her. No one had asked her any questions, and as much as she longed to blame them for being unfriendly, she knew that wasn't the case. Hyacinth had never allowed a normal conversation to develop, one in which she could have spoken of her childhood in Kansas City or her summers in Mumbai with her grandmother. Oh, yes, Hyacinth thought, such natural chatting would have been divine. Suddenly overwhelmed with stories she wished she had shared with the others, Hyacinth cried even harder. And as intense as the tears were, she made a special point to remain as quiet as possible. After all Hyacinth had done that day, she didn't wish to disturb anyone any further.

Downstairs, Madeleine moved about frantically, wildly slapping her arms and legs. She was certain she felt the tickling walk of multiple insects and spiders all across her body. Madeleine's preoccupation with bugs was not a reflection of her indifference to Mrs. Wellington's pain. On the contrary, Madeleine had a sinking pit of misery in her stomach over Mrs. Wellington. But she also recognized that she couldn't ignore the army of spiders and beetles roaming Summerstone.

"I can feel them crawling on me. This is absolute torture," Madeleine said, her voice cracking.

"Miss Madeleine," Schmidty said, "it's awful to see you so distraught. I believe I have some extra repellent stored away for emergencies. Perhaps you would care to wait here while I find it?"

"Oh, yes! That would be brilliant. You are such a lovely man. Thank you," Madeleine said as Schmidty made his way into Summerstone.

"Guys, I'm really battling with something," Garrison said while brushing blond locks away from his tanned face.

"Oh, no! Have they gotten to you too?" Madeleine squealed.

"No, Maddie, and they haven't gotten to you either. It's just your imagination, I promise," Garrison said, lowering his eyes to the ground. "I know it's wrong, because surfers are supposed to be about peace and forgiveness, but I am so angry at that girl. I can't even say her name, I'm just so mad…"

"Don't be so hard on yourself; you're a *pretend* surfer, not a *pretend* Buddhist. You don't have to like everyone," Lulu responded.

"Buddhism is definitely on my list of potential religions," Theo mumbled to himself.

"It's really unfair. Mrs. Wellington doesn't deserve this," Lulu added with a sigh, "and neither do we. If the school is exposed, what happens to us? Who will help us? How could one blabbermouth ten-year-old cause this much trouble? I'm so mad I could cry. And Puncha-lowers don't cry . . . not even at funerals."

"Bartholomews definitely cry. Well, technically, not my mom or my dad or any of my siblings, but I do," Theo said, placing his hand on Lulu's shoulder. "Maybe it's not so bad. Maybe when the article comes out, past students will come forward and tell the reporter about how Mrs. Wellington helped them. And then she can write another article and no one will even remember Abernathy."

"Honestly, I don't think it would matter if others came forward," Madeleine said while spraying repellent all around her. "If you heard that Mrs. Wellington drove a former student into becoming a forest-dwelling nutter, would you trust her with your child?"

"Well, my parents might, but they're not that into me," Lulu mumbled. "Mrs. Wellington is a true wacko, but somehow, against all logic and common sense, she does manage to help people. It really is one of life's great mysteries."

"So that's it? This is Mrs. Wellington's legacy? The crazy lady on the hill who turned a man into an anti-social forest-dweller. Oh, and she matched her makeup to her clothes. No. That is *not* right. I won't accept it," Theo said. He paused to touch his stomach. "Something really creepy is happening. I feel my inner activist coming out."

"Why must you make it seem like an alien is coming out of your stomach just because you feel motivated to help someone?" Lulu asked, rolling her eyes at the theatrical boy.

"I don't believe in aliens, Lulu, you know that. This new persona, the man who doesn't just accept the way things are but changes them, I think he deserves a new name. How about Adam the Activist?"

"You are beginning to sound like someone with multiple personalities."

"Point taken, Lulu, so it's just Theo the Activist. Here's what Theo the Activist is thinking. Let's get a whole bunch of new students and chronicle how Mrs. Wellington cures them. It will be a documentary, which I will host à la Michael Moore. Hosting is something I have always wanted to try, so this would let me kill two birds with one stone. And I say that metaphorically, because as you know, I would never kill a bird, let alone with a stone."

"Sorry, Theo, but I think your national debut is going to have to wait," Garrison chimed in.

"Honestly, Theo, weren't you listening?" Madeleine asked. "No parent in their right mind would send their children to School of Fear once they read that story. We simply won't be able to scrounge up any new nutters for your documentary."

"Nutters would be a great name for a candy bar. Peanuts, walnuts, pecans—all covered in caramel and chocolate. Around Christmas they could do a special macadamia or hazelnut bar... *Holiday Nutter—better for you than cooking with butter*. The slogan needs a little work but you get the idea."

Lulu and Madeleine were staring dumbfounded at Theo when Garrison suddenly started pumping his fist in the air. "Maybe it's not about finding new students, but revisiting an old one?"

CHAPTER 21

EVERYONE'S AFRAID OF SOMETHING:

Novercaphobia is the fear

of stepmothers.

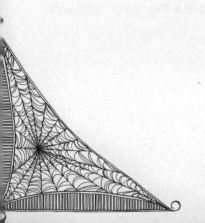

With repellent in hand, Madeleine set about creating a cloud so dense that she could barely make out Garrison seated a mere three feet away. She didn't care that she was essentially bathing in harmful chemicals and solvents. Madeleine could focus on only one thing—or rather two things, spiders and beetles. If she was to reenter the den of doom, as she thought of Summerstone, she needed to take precautions. This was unlike any normal situation: she knew for a fact that there were spiders and beetles in the house, and lots of them.

As Madeleine continued to fret endlessly about spiders and such, Garrison continued with his epiphany. "We need to recruit Abernathy. The article isn't running until the end of the month, so if we can get him here and on the path to rehabilitation it could destroy this woman's article...and maybe she won't run it...or even if she does, it won't be so powerful."

"I am really hoping there is another Abernathy out there in the world, because I am not into hanging out with the weird forest guy," Theo said, shaking his head. "I was actually thinking we should recommend him for a makeover show, get rid of the moss under his nails and stuff. Maybe after that we could hang out, but preferably not in the forest."

"You are so selfish!" Lulu snapped at Theo. "What happened to Theo the Activist? All you think about is yourself. What's best for you? What's easiest for you? When are you going to eat next? And the worst part is, you pretend to be this kind, emotional, sensitive *man*, when you're really just a scared, self-centered little *boy*."

Theo stared at Lulu as Garrison and Madeleine looked away, afraid that Theo might spontaneously combust or drown himself in hysterics. But he didn't. Instead, he took a deep breath, an exceptionally long breath. It was so long, in fact, that it was rather implausible that it was actually all one breath. But that was Theo, always looking to overdo things. After the abnormally and most likely impossible two-minute breath, Theo looked down at his sash. He touched it. He rubbed it against his face, but not to wipe away tears.

"You're right, Lulu," Theo said slowly and in an incredibly calm manner. "I was being selfish and immature, and very unlike a hall monitor, and for that I'm sorry. I take full responsibility for my behavior, because that is what a *man* should do."

"Wow, thanks, Theo," Lulu said with a satisfied smile. "I'm really surprised and even a little impressed."

"Well, that's what I do, I impress people," Theo said with a shrug. "Also, I would like to remind you that at the age of thirteen I am considered in many cultures to be a man, so next time you tell me off, you can just say I am an immature man instead of a boy."

"If you want me to call you a man, then act like one. Help us get Abernathy up here and reenrolled in School of Fear."

"Not to interrupt," Madeleine said softly, "but we don't even know what his phobia is, or if there's only one. Abernathy could have thousands, for all we know. Plus, how exactly do you plan on drawing him out of the forest? Or were you planning to have us enter the forest?"

"OK, we are not entering the forest," Garrison said authoritatively. "The four of us getting lost and disappearing in the vines is not going to help Mrs. Wellington's case. If we go down there, I bet he'll come to the edge and stare at us like he did last summer. From there we need to figure out how to persuade him to come up to Summerstone and reenroll."

"I say we start with a plate of sandwiches and move on to tiramisu, because you know he can't get take-out in the forest."

"Not that I am opposed to taking him a sandwich, or biscuits or sweets, but it's rather imperative that we have a more advanced plan than simply food. Perhaps we should consult Schmidty. The more information on

Abernathy we have, the more likely we are to under-stand what happened between him and Mrs. Welling-ton," Madeleine said intelligently.

"Agreed," Lulu and Garrison said in unison.

"But we're still bringing food, right?"

"Yes, Chubs, there will be food," Lulu said as Schmidty came outside with a tray of cheese, crackers, and fruit.

"I'm afraid it's going to be a cold and rather minimal supper, children. I simply don't have the energy to turn on the stove."

"Yes, yes, of course," Madeleine said sweetly. "But Schmidty, would you mind sitting with us for a moment? We would very much like to pick your brain."

"Please pick away, Miss Madeleine."

"I suppose there is no delicate way to ask this, so I am just going to come out with it. Why was Abernathy origi-nally sent to School of Fear?"

Schmidty nervously patted his comb-over before answering. "Abernathy had a dreadful case, perhaps the worst case in history, of novercaphobia." Schmidty paused to see if that meant anything to them. "The fear of stepmothers."

"This is straight out of a fairy tale," a riveted Theo said as the others looked at him questioningly. "Cinderella. Doesn't anyone read anymore? I'm beginning to feel like the last scholar standing."

"I'm pretty sure that you're sitting down, and you're definitely not a scholar," Lulu clarified.

"It was all much more sad and unfortunate than any fairy tale I've read, and as you know, there was no happy ending for anyone involved."

"I loathe pressing you on this, Schmidty, but we have a plan to help Mrs. Wellington, and we need to know everything. In order for this plan to have even the faintest chance of working, we must know *everything* that happened between Mrs. Wellington and Abernathy," Madeleine said firmly.

"Well, I'm not sure it's my place to discuss another student with you, especially as it's a sensitive case. Madame is already devastated; I would hate for her to feel I betrayed her confidence and Abernathy's."

"Listen, Schmidty, you need a reality check. Mrs. Wellington's name is going to be mud, absolutely ruined. However false the content of this article, it will seem credible because of Abernathy. Unless we do something, the school is finished! It's over! Dead!" Garrison said heatedly. This prompted Schmidty to sit down.

"Yes, I know," the old man said despondently.

"We're trying to help Mrs. Wellington and you. But we need some information," Garrison continued in a slightly softer tone.

"This is a serious long shot, Schmidty, but we need to try. We want to try," Lulu added, "for you and for us. Without School of Fear, who's going to help us?"

"All right, I'll help you, but first, may I inquire what this plan is?"

"We are going to get Abernathy to reenroll in school so Mrs. Wellington can help him get better before the article runs. Without Abernathy living in the forest, it's not such a great story, so maybe the reporter will kill the whole thing," Garrison explained. "And before you even think it, no, we are not entering the forest. We're pretty confident he will come to the edge of the woods to watch us, like he did last summer."

"Since he doesn't have TV in the forest, I bet he thinks of us as a reality show," Theo muttered.

"Children, I think it's terribly kind of you to try to help Madame. I am so touched as well, but I must tell you, this will not work. He will not reenroll in the school, of that I can assure you."

"How can you be so certain?" Lulu asked, annoyed. "Don't you even want to try? Or have you already given up?"

"Schmidty, we're talking about your Madame here. The woman you dote on night and day as if she were your very own flesh and blood. How can you give up so easily?" Garrison said, pushing his blond locks from his face in frustration.

"Oh, I've certainly not given up *easily*, Mister Garrison. I've spent decades trying to lure Abernathy back, to push Madame to make it right with him, but it never works; it is simply a lost cause. It's an awful lesson in the harsh realities of life, but I am afraid not all wrongs can be corrected, no matter how hard we try."

"Schmidty, I simply cannot comprehend any of this, and I'm regarded as terribly clever. Please, you must explain the entire story from the beginning. We need to understand why you think our chances are so bleak," Madeleine implored.

"Yes, I suppose you do need to understand. It all began when Abernathy's mother died just shy of his second birthday. As an only child, he grew increasingly close and emotionally dependent on his father. Abernathy absolutely worshipped the man. The two were utterly inseparable. And in Abernathy's mind, it never occurred to him that it would ever be any different. It wasn't until he started primary school that he even learned that widowers often remarried.

"He felt threatened that an imaginary woman might take his father away, and he became terrified of any age-appropriate woman speaking to his father. The boy was completely obsessed. The only women in his father's age bracket he deemed suitable for dinners or parties were blood relations. And you can imagine how tedious life becomes when your only friends are blood related."

"Did his father even want to remarry? Was he actively seeking another wife?" Madeleine asked.

"Oh, no. On the contrary, he promised Abernathy he would never marry again, but still the boy worried. He even became phobic of other people's stepmothers, ending friendships with anyone who had a stepmother or even liked a stepmother or spoke to a stepmother. It was at this time that his father decided something had to be done, that it had become a life-impairing problem. Why, the boy stopped attending his math class when he learned that Mrs. Elfin herself was a stepmother. And Mrs. Elfin was such a lovely woman..."

"So his dad brought him to School of Fear?" Lulu prodded Schmidty, in an effort to keep the story on track.

"Yes, but at that time School of Fear was based in New York City. Of course, School of Fear was not his first stop. Abernathy's father had gone through a slew of other things, like counselors, hypnotists, shamans, even a very short-lived fad known as clown therapy—"

"I'm sorry to interrupt, especially since it takes Schmidty so long to tell a story—which, by the way, is not an insult, just a comment," Theo said with an oblivious smile. "OK, you and Mrs. Wellington say a lot of cuckoo stuff, and most of the time I just let it fly right by. But in this case, I can't do it. I cannot go on with my life or your story without knowing—what is clown therapy?"

"I suppose you are too young to remember it. It was awfully controversial in its day," Schmidty explained. "The Union of Clowns and Mimes protested the clown therapy headquarters for seven months straight. Claimed it was defamatory to clowns everywhere."

"Yes, but what was it?" Theo persisted.

"Clown therapy was based on the premise that if a clown terrified a child, completely spooked him out of his gourd, the child would become so phobic of clowns that he or she would entirely forget his other fear. For rather obvious reasons, it wasn't terribly successful. However, as it turns out, one of the clowns was actually a former student of Madame's, and he was the one who told Abernathy's father of the highly secretive institution on the Upper East Side, School of Fear."

"OK, enough about clown therapy," Lulu said impatiently. "We need to know more about Abernathy."

"Yes, please, Schmidty," Madeleine said with a tense smile. "And it's already terribly late, and as you know, we *must,* without question, fumigate Summerstone before bed."

"Haven't any of you ever wondered what Abernathy's surname is?" Schmidty asked pointedly.

"The guy lives in the forest. I doubt he flosses his teeth on a regular basis," Theo said. "So I don't think he's using his last name for much."

Schmidty cleared his throat before speaking. "Abernathy Wellington."

CHAPTER 22

EVERYONE'S AFRAID OF SOMETHING:

Hylophobia is the fear

of forests.

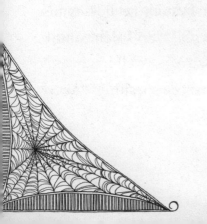
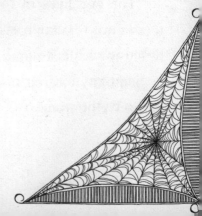

Madeleine, Lulu, Garrison, and Theo didn't say a word. Why, they didn't even nod their heads; they simply waited to hear more. This was quite a revelation, and they needed time to process what this meant for their mission. Compassion, confusion, and so much more raced through the children's heads as they pondered what life would be like with Mrs. Wellington as a stepmother. For in truth, each had taken quite a while to warm to the woman as their teacher.

Schmidty continued. "Love at first sight is such a wondrous and magical occurrence, but in this case it was also fraught with pain and misery. The first time Madame saw Harold and Harold saw Madame, they both knew. It struck them like a truck on the road, just bowled them over. Of course, as Mrs. Wellington was Abernathy's teacher, they both fought it tooth and nail. But fighting against love only makes it stronger. With each stolen glance or brush of the hand, their love blossomed. Around this time, Abernathy actually began to make progress under Mrs. Wellington's—or rather, Ms. Hesterfield's, as she was known then—tutelage. He even started attending Mrs. Elfin's class again; it was the most wondrous of changes.

"Madame and Abernathy's father were so struck by the transformation, they both vowed never to act on their love, for the young boy's sake. These proclamations, among many others, were made in letters the two exchanged. But as I always say, if you write it, someone will surely read it, and Abernathy did just that. And the letter he happened upon was, well, the most romantic of them all, filled with the stuff of movies, a love that couldn't be stopped but also could never be fulfilled..."

"Then what happened?" Madeleine asked, with all the excitement she had felt during her first reading of *Pride and Prejudice*.

"The boy combusted, turned himself inside out. And at this point the two decided that marriage was best. Since Abernathy knew, and the damage was done, they decided they ought to marry and conquer the situation as a family matter, not as a school matter. However well-meaning the plan was, it didn't unfold very well. Abernathy ran away constantly, ending up in dangerous parts of the city, alone on bus benches or sitting at lunch counters. Madame and Harold agreed that perhaps it would be good for Abernathy to have a country retreat, a place where he could run around outside without any concerns, and so Summerstone was built."

"Did it help?" Garrison asked, intrigued. "Did he chill out?"

"Not really. The boy never spent one night in the house. He wouldn't share a roof with his father or step-mother...he refused...so for much of the time he simply ran wild on the grounds, sleeping in trees and in flower beds. School of Fear was still located in the city at this time, and Madame and Harold would commute to Summerstone for the weekends, where they would work tirelessly to break through to Abernathy."

"Wait. They left him alone at Summerstone as a kid?" Lulu asked.

"He was a teenager by then, and he had a caretaker— myself—and a tutor."

"Who was the tutor?" Theo asked.

"A very odd Dutch man, who I might add was not very intelligent, but then again, it's not easy to find top tutors willing to conduct lessons in trees. Anyway, Madame continued to cure student after student, but she never made any progress with Abernathy. And as the years wore on, she tried less. It was the day before Abernathy's eighteenth birthday that Harold died on the train on his way up here. Harold grabbed his chest, mentioned how he wished he had time to get his hair trimmed, and then boom—he was dead. At the funeral, Abernathy sat two plots away in a large oak tree. Few people even knew he was there. After that, he disappeared. Occasionally there would be sightings of him in national parks or forests. Eventually Madame moved the school to Summerstone, and maybe twice we thought we might have seen him near the forest, but we were never certain. It had been so long, and he had aged so poorly. Then, last summer, he arrived and, well, you know the rest."

"How does he survive? What does he eat? How does he get any money?" Garrison asked.

"We haven't the faintest idea," Schmidty confessed. "Children, I won't stop you from going tomorrow, for I think it the kindest, most wonderful thing anyone has ever attempted on Madame's behalf. However, I must ask you not to mention a word of it to Madame. Since success is more than a long shot, I can't bear the idea of upsetting her even more."

"Of course, Schmidty," Lulu said. "We won't say a word."

"I must retire now; this day has more than taken its toll on me. I hope you understand, Miss Madeleine, how much I wish I was up for spider and beetle corralling, but I am simply too drained by the day's events."

"I most certainly understand, Schmidty. And thank you so much for sharing that story with us. We will work our absolute hardest to bring Abernathy home tomorrow," Madeleine said with a smile. Her cheeks flushed, and she lowered her eyes. "Oh, and Schmidty, should you remember any more details of Mr. and Mrs. Wellington's love letters, feel free to share them with me—only if appropriate, of course."

"Jeesh, Maddie," Theo said, shaking his head. "Don't they have the Lifetime channel in London?"

"Oh, Theo," Madeleine said huffily, "your idea of romance is a cheese sandwich and crisps."

Theo did not dispute this fact. In truth, he would prefer a sandwich to almost anything—except safety, of course.

"Goodnight, children. I'll see you first thing tomorrow morning." And with that the old man waddled away.

With Schmidty's departure, Madeleine's romance-riddled brain snapped back to attention and she began smothering herself in repellent again. She sprayed and sprayed and sprayed and sprayed until she was literally drenched.

"Maddie, I'm dying here," Garrison whined. "Seriously, I'm developing asthma from sitting next to you."

"Don't joke about asthma, Garrison," Theo said harshly. "It's a very serious condition, and I should know. My cat has it; he has a little kitty inhaler and everything."

260

"Enough about asthma and your cat," Lulu snapped. "All he meant was that Maddie needs to stop spraying. It's too much. There are puddles of repellent around her shoes."

"There are one hundred massive brown-and-burgundy spiders inside, and one hundred beetles. I cannot take any chances. The only hope I have is to exude repellent from my pores. I haven't been spraying in almost a year. I don't have the buildup in my system that I once did. Do you realize what I am facing? It's an army of creepy-crawlers!"

"Don't worry, Madeleine, we are totally going to catch them all," Lulu said. "I mean, Summerstone isn't that big..."

"Plus, there are only ninety-nine spiders, because you killed one on your head, remember?"

"Yes, Theo, I do remember—quite vividly, as a matter of fact," Madeleine responded as a shiver ran up her spine.

"Me too. That imprint was so detailed, kind of like a photograph on your forehead. All the tiny hairs on the spider's legs, the weird bumps, the eyes...you could see everything," Theo said slowly.

"Theo, stop talking," Lulu protested, shaking her head at the chubby boy.

"Yeah, that's probably a good idea."

As soon as Theo closed his mouth, a sweaty-faced Madeleine leaned to her left and vomited.

"Oh, dear, I am so embarrassed. That must have been dreadful for all of you. I assure you I would have moved had I had the time..." Madeleine trailed off, her cheeks rosy.

"Maddie, it wasn't your fault. It wasn't even *my* fault. Lulu clearly should have stopped me earlier," Theo said judgmentally, as the group migrated away from the stench.

"Don't start with me, Chunker. I'm tired and hungry, and we are very close to a cliff."

"Point taken," Theo said quietly.

"Thank heavens you haven't regressed too much, Maddie. Imagine if you had gone all crazy like last summer?" Lulu said sarcastically, watching Madeleine fiddle with her shower cap and veil.

"Honestly, Lulu, you really can be a sour girl. And might I remind you that you yourself do not ride alone in elevators, and even on occasion fake going to the loo to mislead your parents?"

"Guess I kind of deserved that. Sorry," Lulu said, looking down.

"This whole thing is dreadful. Frankly, I cannot understand how I'm even in this scenario. How on earth did this happen to me?" Madeleine asked the group rhetorically.

"Hyacinth, the Knapps, bad luck... pretty much covers it all," Theo said as he paused to put his hand on his chest. "I think that cheese is repeating on me. Does that happen to anyone else?"

Everyone stared at Theo, unsure how he managed to get the conversation to this point.

"Maddie, the good news is that Schmidty already captured fourteen beetles and seventeen spiders," Garrison explained to a distraught Madeleine.

"Oh, how lovely! Did he kill them? Is he positive they are deceased?"

"He put them back in their jars, and triple-checked that the lids were closed tightly."

"Very well," Madeleine said with mild disappointment. "Although I cannot promise such compassion should any of them come within spraying distance."

"Got it," Garrison said with a nod of the head. "Are we ready, then?"

"Shouldn't we stretch or something first?" Theo asked. "Maybe a little warmup? Discuss trapping techniques?"

"Theo, this isn't the Olympics. It's not going to be that strenuous or complicated. You see a spider or a beetle, throw it in a small jar, then transport it back to the B and B and mark the tally," Garrison said.

"Wow, I expected more out of you, Garrison. I thought team captains were known for their pep talks. No wonder you guys didn't take state in basketball this year. What did you tell your teammates — *'Hey, it's just a ball, get it in the net'?*" Theo said in a high-pitched girly voice.

"First of all, I don't sound like that. And you want a pep talk?" Garrison said with exponentially growing annoyance. "Fine!" he continued, running his fingers through his long blond locks and closing his eyes. When he reopened them, a cooler, calmer, more collected Garrison had emerged. "This is a challenge, one of many we will face in the next twenty-four hours. But when we go out there, whether it be to find bugs or to find Abernathy, we cannot worry about ourselves. We cannot think about our own sacrifices, for we are doing this for our friends, Madeleine and Mrs. Wellington. We will catch these spiders and beetles because Madeleine needs us to. We will do this for her because she's our friend, and a good one at that. No, I take that back, she's a *great* one. And so is Mrs. Wellington."

"That was beautiful, just beautiful. I'd like you to give the eulogy at my funeral, should you outlive me," Theo said, dabbing his eyes.

"Way to be weird, Theo," Lulu said as she started toward the massive front door. "Let's do this. We don't have much time if we're going to get any sleep before tomorrow."

Lulu entered the foyer quietly, tiptoeing across the wooden planks. Theo, directly behind her, plopped around noisily, banging things with his hands as he walked.

"Theo, stop being so loud. You'll frighten them away," Lulu whispered.

"Or frighten them *out* of their hiding spots? Lulu,

don't worry about me. I've got plans. Or rather *a* plan. And everyone knows you need only one good plan. I've got mine—make some noise, draw them out of their comfort zones, then swoop in. But no killing. That doesn't work with my whole vegetarian thing..."

"Will you stop talking and start catching?" Lulu said as she pushed Theo toward the Great Hall.

"I got one," Garrison said loudly as he pushed a large brown-and-burgundy spider into his jar.

"I feel a bit green," Madeleine said when she saw the large furry creature. "Perhaps I'll wait outside with Macaroni. We really haven't had much time for a proper catchup," she said as she ran back to the front door.

Garrison figured the spiders and beetles would only have been able to squeeze into rooms with doors that were either ajar or had a wide space between the floor and the door bottom. This narrowed the list down to the ballroom, the Library of Smelly Foods, the kitchen, dining room, polo field, and living quarters. Lulu took the foyer and upstairs, while Theo and Garrison started on the rooms off the Great Hall.

Lulu was extraordinarily fast at seeing and snapping up beetles. Knowing their proclivity for hiding in plain sight, she instantly caught an astonishing twenty-five on the pageant photos, most of them posing as earrings, hair clips, or brooches. (The bulk of this find was a double-wrap necklace made out of eleven beetles.) Shortly thereafter Lulu discovered nineteen beetles framing a small painting, six on Madeleine's favorite polka-dot pullover, and eight on the black squares on the chessboard in the boys' room. Lulu had impressively found fifty-eight in all, bringing the grand total to seventy-two captured beetles. Unfortunately, she wasn't so lucky on the spider front. Lulu was able to find only four in the hall closet upstairs and three in the foyer.

Theo and Garrison started in the kitchen—not surprisingly, at Theo's recommendation. As Garrison peered into the pink cupboards and under the magenta stove, Theo looked through a loaf of sliced bread, eating two pieces in the process. He followed the bread with shoving a handful of crackers into his mouth. Soon crumbs were cascading off his chubby cheeks and down the front of his shirt.

"Would you stop eating? I need help," Garrison barked.

"Excuse me, Gary, but I'm helping. There could have

been beetles or spiders in the bread or crackers. It's not like they don't eat carbs."

"How do you know you didn't eat one without realizing it? I mean, you barely chew."

Theo immediately stopped chewing. He wanted to spit the food out, but worried what he would see. He wasn't concerned that he could have eaten a spider, as they were too big to miss, but a beetle was an entirely different matter. They were small enough, and Theo imagined they crunched a lot like a cracker. With a pained expression, Theo swallowed the lump of food in his mouth. Whatever was in there, he didn't want to know. "Yeah, maybe this wasn't the best time for a snack," a queasy-faced Theo acquiesced.

"Let's check the dining room," Garrison said as he walked toward the beaded doorway that connected it with the kitchen.

"Wow, they are smart," Theo said as he stared at the pink strands of beads that hung between the two rooms. The beetles had formed a *V* shape across the beads, looking much like a purposeful design.

"Lulu thinks they're smarter than you are," Garrison said with a grin.

"I take that as a compliment," Theo said huffily, then paused. "On second thought, I don't!"

After running through the Library of Smelly Foods and the polo field, Theo and Garrison had yet to find one spider. They did, however, add to the sixteen beetles they'd found in the kitchen, finding another eight hidden on different parts of the horses, from eyes to nostrils to the unmentionables.

As the boys headed for the classroom, they noticed a dim light shining beneath a nondescript door next to the Greenland Fungus room. It wasn't a beautiful, weird, or scary door; it was so utterly normal that it could have been found in any house in America.

"Look, there's a light on," Garrison said, as he moved toward the plain door, much to Theo's irritation.

"Let's stay on track, OK? We are on bug duty. Then we have Abernathy tomorrow. We have a seriously packed schedule, and as it is, I'm feeling a little overwhelmed...hey, wait! What are you doing?" Theo nervously asked as Garrison quietly opened the door.

"Stay here," Garrison whispered to Theo.

"No way! We're a team! We're Tharrison! Or Gareo!"

"No name combining," Garrison whispered as he started down a dark, wood-paneled hall. The dimly lit corridor opened up into a proper library with books, a fireplace, a wall of trophies, and more pictures than one could count. There were framed photos of children, adults, and families all over the room — above the fireplace and on the mantel, the bookshelf, the end tables, and hanging on the walls.

"Who is there?" Mrs. Wellington asked in a commanding voice.

The tall back of her leather chair obstructed the boys' view of Mrs. Wellington, and vice versa.

"Garrison and Theo," Garrison announced uneasily, nervous that they were about to get into trouble for snooping.

"Students from your school," Theo added awkwardly. "We didn't mean to interrupt. It's just that we noticed a light on while we were bug hunting. And since we don't like to waste energy, we came in here to turn it off. So please don't be upset. We thought we were helping the environment… *let's not fight over a silly light*… I just made that slogan up… it's not my best work, but I think you get the idea —" Theo blustered.

"Look at all these faces, all these lives I've helped. Quite remarkable, isn't it? And soon none of it will matter," Mrs. Wellington interrupted Theo, completely disregarding the conversation on conservation.

"That's not true," Theo responded. "Look at all your trophies. Speaking as someone who has never won a trophy, they really matter... they make you important... and no one can take that away from you."

"I've won more trophies than I can count," Garrison said, before noticing Theo's envious expression. "So where did all these trophies come from?"

"We used to play other schools—specialty schools like the Fibbers' Academy, Silent School, the Awkward Institute, Contrary Conservatory—but now there are hardly any left. People are too afraid, too afraid of being found out, and lied about, and sued, and ruined," Mrs. Wellington said as she stood up and walked toward the boys. "And conceivably with good reason. The world is not what it used to be."

"OK, this isn't good," Garrison mumbled.

"No, it certainly isn't, but there is nothing left to do, except perhaps die," Mrs. Wellington said as she approached the boys. "I suppose I should start planning my funeral, picking out the dress, getting my wig ready, finding worm-proof makeup, and of course, decorating the casket. I'm thinking a pink exterior with a lavender lining. Or maybe I should do solid gold. After all, you only die once..."

"Mrs. Wellington, we are more than happy to help with the casket decoration, but right now there's another more pressing situation," Theo babbled while stepping away from his teacher. "Way, way, way more pressing situation."

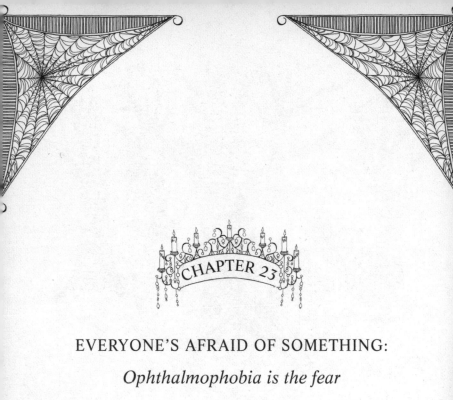

CHAPTER 23

EVERYONE'S AFRAID OF SOMETHING:

Ophthalmophobia is the fear

of being stared at.

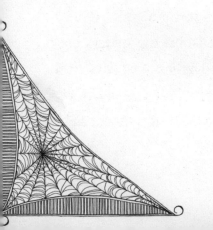

Poor Mrs. Wellington, so distraught and distressed, had failed to notice that her shawl was in fact a blanket of brown-and-burgundy spiders. The spiders had interlocked their legs with one another, creating a rather sophisticated-looking knit. It was all quite a blessing, as it was terribly easy to transport the spiders back to the B and B while clustered together. And Mrs. Wellington hardly seemed to notice or mind that she was wearing a mass of spiders. She was far too inconsolable about the school to care about such a trivial thing. When all was said and done, only four beetles were unaccounted for, and Theo was beginning to think he may have eaten at least two in his haste to inhale the crackers.

After a detailed search of the girls' bedroom and bathroom, Madeleine was finally able to fall asleep, albeit in her shower cap, veil, and rain poncho, with a can of repellent in each hand. Nearby, Lulu tossed and turned with vivid dreams of dogs tap dancing and singing show tunes. Next door, Theo lay awake most of the night with his hands on his stomach. The contractions in his lower intestine left him with little doubt that he had indeed eaten a beetle or two. His mind teemed with images of half-chewed beetles gnawing on his organs or, worse, procreating.

Theo longed to wake Garrison and get another pep talk, maybe one about putting aside your own internal insect farm to help your teacher, but he refrained. Garrison was sleeping far too soundly to wake him. The ability to sleep before a big day must be the result of years of sports tournaments, Theo thought.

Across the hall, Hyacinth awoke in the middle of the

night confused and disoriented. As she sat up in bed, it all came rushing back to her. Her heart again dropped into her stomach as she remembered the terrible events that had transpired. Though impressed that she had actually been able to fall asleep while alone in a room, she was still in the grip of rampant panic. The extreme silence of the room left her with a pounding heart and racing thoughts.

What would her life be like if she were *always* alone? Would she be forced to live with the horrible, suffocating fright she was currently experiencing? The young girl hopped out of bed and threw on a clean green pantsuit. With sweaty palms she slowly turned the knob of her bedroom door. Hyacinth listened with all her might for some small sound from the others. She just needed proof that she wasn't actually all alone in this enormous mansion. But she heard nothing. It was, after all, 4:00 AM. She slid to the floor and waited for the sun to rise, for confirmation that the others were still there.

When Madeleine, Lulu, Garrison, and Theo tiptoed into the hall at 6:45, Hyacinth covertly watched from her room. Simply seeing the others flooded her with a sense of joy and reassurance, but it also magnified the estrangement she had caused. Hyacinth slipped into the kitchen while the others held an extremely early breakfast/strategy session with Schmidty. She eavesdropped as the group decided that Macaroni would not accompany them on the Abernathy adventure, due to his aversion to the feel of cobblestones on his paws. Also, bulldogs are not known for their communication skills, so all agreed it was best to leave him at Summerstone. The rules set forth by Schmidty were simple: do not enter the woods. The students were only allowed to call Abernathy's name from the edge of the forest, and if the man appeared, to plead with him to come up to Summerstone.

"You know I loathe to be the naysayer," Schmidty explained, "the voice of gloom and doom, especially since I am so touched by all that you are doing to help Madame, but I simply don't want you to feel disappointed or responsible should he not return with you. This is a man who has been alone for most of his life, living outside in the wilderness, away from society. He won't be the easiest of candidates to convince."

"But Abernathy came out before; he could do it again," Garrison offered. "We have to try. We can't just let Mrs. Wellington sit here and wait to die. She is a good teacher and she has helped a lot of people, and if she could help Abernathy, then we might be able to stop that article."

"Gary, I've never known you to be so optimistic and driven. I'll be honest; I am really inspired right now. If we were near a field, I think I could play a few rounds of some sport," Theo said proudly.

"A few rounds of some sport," Lulu repeated wryly. "You don't even know how to talk about sports, let alone play them."

"And I'm not even going to start with you on the Gary thing," Garrison muttered.

"Schmidty, do you think Abernathy will be frightened by my ensemble? Is it best I stay here?" Madeleine asked politely.

"Don't try to get out of this, Maddie," Lulu said decisively. "Plus, remember, there are still four beetles loose in Summerstone, so you're not truly safe anywhere."

"Thank you for those unpleasant and distressing words, Lulu," Madeleine said through gritted teeth.

"No problem," Lulu said with a smile. "So Abernathy is afraid of stepmothers, and none of us have stepmothers. Yeah, this is going to be a piece of cake."

"Positive energy, Lulu! Mrs. Wellington needs us. This school is it for her, so the least we can do is try to help," Theo pleaded. "Anyway, who's going to help us if she's not here?"

"You're right, Chubby. Let's do this," Lulu said as she stood up from the table.

"And everyone is absolutely positive that I should come?" Madeleine asked nervously.

"Four supersmart beetles, Maddie, and we have no idea where they are," Garrison said with a smile.

"Right," Madeleine said with a tense expression. "Let's find Abernathy."

"I'm ready with sandwiches and tiramisu. What are you guys bringing?" Theo asked the others.

"Our brains," Lulu deadpanned. "And hopefully, a lot of luck."

While Abernathy sometimes came up to Summerstone, the group thought the odds of finding him were better if they went to the forest. Theo, Madeleine, Garrison, and Lulu took an uneventful trip down the mountain in the SVT; why, Theo didn't even do a set of stretches afterward. He simply walked off the tram like the rest of them. And there the group stood staring at the massive walls of foliage bordering the forest. It wasn't an insanely long time that the foursome stood there staring, but it felt like it to them. Each of them wondered how on earth they would be able to lure Abernathy to the edge, let alone entice him up to the school and persuade him to reenroll. The mission to save Mrs. Wellington suddenly felt very much like an exercise in futility.

"So I'm thinking maybe we sing a song, set a friendly mood, to start this off," Theo said, breaking the silence.

"A song?" Lulu asked incredulously. "What do you think this is, a musical?"

"What about something festive, like the national anthem?"

"I'm not sure I know that song, Theo, and I'm actually not too keen on my voice," Madeleine said sweetly while covering herself in repellent.

"Theo, no one is singing. And we certainly aren't singing the national anthem to a man living in the forest," Lulu shot back.

"And for all we know, the national anthem's changed since he was a kid," Garrison offered.

Lulu, Theo, and Madeleine all looked at Garrison and shook their heads.

"Fine. Maybe it hasn't changed," Garrison said with embarrassment. "It's not like I'm listening to it on my iPod. How was I supposed to know?"

"Moving on, should I display the food, sort of like a buffet on the ground?"

"How about we start by calling his name?" Garrison offered.

"Won't that insult him, like he's some lost dog or something?" Lulu responded quickly.

"No way. People call my name all the time on the field, and I never think of myself as a dog. Just don't say it all singsongy, like a dog's name."

"I never realized it until now, but my whole family says my name in that singsongy lost-pet voice. *Theeeeeoooooo!* What do you think it means? Lack of respect, or display of affection?"

"OK, Theo, get a therapist. Garrison, call his name. Maddie, keep spraying yourself," Lulu said in an unyielding and take-charge manner.

"Abernathy!" Garrison called out.

"We come in peace!" Theo shouted. "We don't bear

gifts, but we do have sandwiches and tiramisu, which are better than most of the gifts I get and I assume better than most gifts you get. Although I'm not sure you even get any gifts without a real mailing address, so..."

"I think it's safe to say that this isn't going very well," Lulu observed.

The foursome stood there looking at the seemingly endless greenery, responsibility weighing heavily on their shoulders. This was it. This was their one and only idea to save Mrs. Wellington, her legacy, and themselves. And there was simply no denying that they were failing. Garrison tried to take a deep breath but he couldn't — and not simply because of Madeleine's repellent. He was too tied up with anxiety and a sense of duty. And he wasn't the only one. Lulu felt a familiar pulsing sensation behind her left eye as the fear of failure took hold.

Madeleine sprayed and sprayed, worrying that she heard insect wings flapping in the distance. And rather predictably, Theo was nervously stealing bites of the sandwiches in the bag. He always ate when he was nervous or happy or bored or, more aptly, awake.

"Um, guys! Look at my head. Is there a light-bulb shining? Because I have an idea!" Theo squealed excitedly. "Here's the plan. Gary, Lulu, Maddie, get behind me in a straight line."

"I have a feeling I'm going to regret whatever it is we're about to do," Garrison mumbled to Madeleine.

"Highly probable," Madeleine agreed.

"This is a supersimple background setup. I want you guys to step side to side and clap your hands in unison. Do you think you can handle that?"

After the requisite eye rolling and scoffing, the three of them begrudgingly began to step and clap.

"Give me an *A!* Give me a *B!* Give me an *E!* Give me an *R!*" Theo cheered as he clumsily executed some rudimentary cheerleader moves. "Give me an *N!* Give me an *A!* Give me a *T!* Give me an *H!* Give me a *Y!* What's that spell? Abernathy! Yeah! Yeah! Abernathy!"

Theo finished his cheer by throwing his imaginary pom-poms in the air and jumping up and down. With a proud smile, he turned back toward his friends, who were bent over one another in hysterics. As his smile faded Theo genuinely began to reconsider his long-held plan to join the cheer squad in high school. This was hardly the reaction he had been expecting.

"That's OK, you guys can totally laugh. It's supposed

to be a comedic routine...seriously...I did it to get this reaction...I thought it would be a good team-building exercise for everyone to laugh at me...honestly, I wasn't being serious...OK, maybe I was, but don't tell Joaquin about this, OK?" Theo babbled.

"You just made my summer," Lulu choked out between tears of laughter. "I can't believe you threw your pretend pom-poms in the air!"

Madeleine suddenly stopped laughing and spraying. The delicate young girl lightly tapped Garrison and Lulu on the shoulders before pointing toward the forest with a smile.

"I underestimated you, Theo," Garrison said kindly. "It worked."

Theo turned triumphantly toward the forest and scanned the dense foliage until he came across Abernathy's ashy face, which was worn and patchy, with crevices scattered across his cheeks. Normally the sight of such a ragged man would send shivers up Theo's spine, but in this instance all he felt was relief. Throwing his imaginary pom-poms in the air once again, he slowly approached the edge of the forest.

"Hi!" Theo shouted out agreeably. "I'm really glad

you were able to catch my performance. Unfortunately I can't do an encore, because those were the only moves I know. So please don't clap or hold up a lighter, because I am fresh out of groove." He paused to smile victoriously at the others. "Anyway, I am here to *officially* tell you that I get it. I would wig out, no pun intended, if Mrs. Wellington were my stepmother. I'm not sure I would go so far as to live in the forest, but I would be really upset.

"However, eventually I'd realize that all of Mrs. Wellington's wackiness, insane behavior, and slights about my weight—well, that's all love. So in the words of the great singing legend Diana Ross, stop in the name of love, and come on up the hill...that second line isn't actually in the song, but you get the general idea—"

"Hello there," Madeleine interrupted. "I'm Madeleine Masterson, and while I don't have a stepmother, I do have a stepgran. It's my father's stepmother, and, well, she's lovely. I consider her to be my grandmother..."

Abernathy continued to stare at the group, much as one would if one didn't speak their language. The man showed absolutely no signs of comprehension or emotion.

"We know you're afraid of her, but she really can help you," Garrison pleaded with Abernathy. "I know how hard that is to believe. Sometimes even I have trouble believing it myself, but it's true...she's helped all of us."

"Abernathy," Theo chimed in, "if I may, I'm going to tell you a little story, man to man—or as the Spanish say, mano a mano—"

"Theo, you do know that mano a mano actually means hand to hand, not man to man, as it is often mis-understood," Madeleine explained. "So unless you're planning on holding Abernathy's hand, that is not the correct phrase."

"Yeah, OK, let's call off the whole mano a mano thing until we have some Purell—no offense Abernathy. And it's not because you live in the forest that I don't want to hold hands. It's more to do with all the colds going around this time of year," Theo rattled on uncom-fortably. "Anyway, like I was saying, when I first arrived at Summerstone I wanted to leave, and on an express train, if you know what I mean. But then I got to know Mrs. Wellington, and then she faked her own death, and that really helped me. It disturbed me too...but it was useful...so basically, I think she could help you.

"I mean, aren't you tired of eating twigs and bugs? Don't you want to order take-out and watch cable television? It's a great life...let us help you discover it. Why don't you follow us up to the house for some tea and cookies, maybe even a little nap, because I don't know about you, but I didn't sleep well last night. By the way, I may have eaten multiple beetles yesterday, and it really freaked me out, and I don't mean any offense by that if you eat beetles—because you live in the forest, what else are you going to eat?"

"Theo—" Madeleine attempted to stop him.

"...Maybe a squirrel, but I truly hope not, because they are pretty cute, not that cuteness should have anything to do with who lives or who dies, but let's be honest it does, that's why we step on spiders and not Chihuahuas..."

"Theo, let's wrap it up," Lulu said quietly.

"Anyway, you're afraid...we're afraid...it's like camp, only really weird...and run by your stepmother who you are terrified of...but I think I speak for the whole group when I say we're all a little terrified of her too. So what do you say?"

Abernathy continued to stare at them.

"Maybe we should just throw the tiramisu at him, to give him a taste of the good life," Theo whispered to the others.

"Hey, I'm Lulu, and I think, of this group, I understand how you feel the most. My mother is more like an alien than a mom to me, and sometimes I wonder what I'm missing out on, what other people have...and it makes me sort of angry...at her...at life...and that's OK. It's OK to be scared or angry, but it's no way to live forever. Let us help you."

Abernathy stared at Lulu. For a second the words seemed to have penetrated; the man truly appeared ready to venture out of the forest. Then, in the blink of an eye, Abernathy was gone. And with him went the only chance of saving Mrs. Wellington and School of Fear.

CHAPTER 24

EVERYONE'S AFRAID OF SOMETHING:

Asthenophobia is the fear

of weakness.

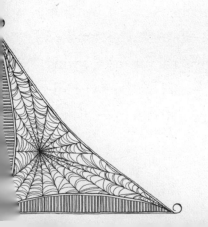

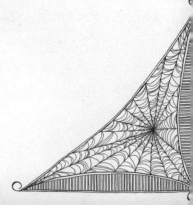

Darkness is not merely the absence of light, but the destruction of hope. Long before night fell, Madeleine, Lulu, Theo, and Garrison had been enveloped in absolute darkness. There was a sense that they had failed at the most important challenge of their lives; an unbelievable burden to carry before having finished puberty. But there they stood, staring at the trees, saying silent prayers that Abernathy would reappear while knowing that he wouldn't. It wasn't that they would never bounce back from this experience; they would. As time moved on, the pain of this failure would fade for each of them. This they knew, even at that moment. Although it wasn't an articulate thought in their heads, they could feel it in their bodies.

One might think that this realization would lessen the pain of the moment; in fact, it only exacerbated it. There they stood with their lives ahead of them, while Mrs. Wellington's life, almost entirely behind her, was sure to be destroyed. There was a tragic element to the entire scenario, from Abernathy to Mrs. Wellington, that simply couldn't be ignored: two pained souls unable to mend.

Not long after 8:00 PM, comets of fireflies began to whip past the students. The realization that even if Abernathy returned they wouldn't be able to see him forced the foursome into the SVT to return empty-handed to Summerstone. They were greeted by Macaroni and Schmidty at the front door. Schmidty didn't ask if the mission was successful, for he knew it wasn't. In fact he had known from the beginning that it wouldn't be, that it was truly a mission impossible.

"Children, I have supper waiting in the dining room,"

Schmidty said sweetly. "Macaroni has already eaten—you know how fussy he can be when hungry—but I've waited, as has Miss Hyacinth and Celery."

"Oh, great," Lulu moaned. "Just what we need: Hyacinth." Stony-faced, she walked into the foyer, where she leaned on the table and waited for the others to filter in.

"Now, we mustn't be rude, Miss Lulu."

"Fine," Lulu acquiesced, emotionally exhausted by her day.

"Schmidty, will Mrs. Wellington be joining us?" Madeleine asked hopefully as she closed the front door behind her. "I would very much like to tell her how much I respect her and that even though I've had a bit of a setback due in part to the double and triple *B*'s, she gave me such a gift this past year. While not cured, I lived an awfully normal existence. No one referred to me as the Veiled Wonder or Spraying Silly. I was simply Madeleine."

"Oh, what lovely words. I shall pass them on to Mrs. Wellington, or if you would like, you may leave her a note. She's taken to her bed and will not be able to say her goodbyes tomorrow when the sheriff comes for you."

"What?" Theo asked. "That's it? We're going home? But we're not ready! Maddie is seriously not ready— she's wearing a shower cap!"

"I know, Mister Theo, but Madame is unable to teach anyone. Why, she's currently unable even to leave her bed, and I am afraid I haven't the skills or stamina to teach you all. But not to worry, your parents will be getting full refunds along with letters explaining the situation, so none of you will be blamed for a lack of progress."

"I don't even know what to say," Garrison said despondently. "I'm really bummed out. I was hoping that one day I might actually be a surfer who surfed."

"Yes, well, sometimes things don't end as we want them to, but that mustn't stop you from moving forward, charging toward life," Schmidty said as he turned toward the Great Hall. "Let's have a nice meal and talk of happy times to come."

"We really can't say goodbye to Mrs. Wellington?" Theo asked with tears in his eyes. "I don't care if she's bald and yellow and scary-looking..."

"I'm afraid not."

Hyacinth was seated at the dining room table with Celery perched on her left shoulder. She nodded as Madeleine, Lulu, Garrison, Theo, and Schmidty entered and took their seats. As calm as she appeared on the surface, the young girl was utterly euphoric to be in the presence of people again, even if they were mad at her.

Schmidty had prepared a delicious dinner of salad, baked ziti, and garlic cauliflower, yet no one seemed able to do more than push the food around their plates.

"Dinner is most scrumptious, Schmidty," Madeleine said politely as she forced a small bite of pasta into her mouth. "Absolutely delicious."

"Yes, Celery and I find it very tasty," Hyacinth said meekly, an opening that was immediately met by an angry glare from Lulu. It was simply too difficult for Lulu to hear Hyacinth's voice without remembering what the little girl had done.

Theo put down his fork and started to cry. It wasn't his usual dramatic fare, with gasps of air and rampant nose-blowing. This was a much more dignified and honest cry. In fact it wasn't even a cry at all, more of a soft weep.

"I don't feel right leaving you and Mrs. Wellington up here alone, rotting away until death finally drags you from this earth. That is not how you are supposed to spend your golden years, or platinum years, or whatever years you guys are in. Why don't you come and live with me? Joaquin wants to get his own place anyway. You and Macaroni could bunk with me, and we'll give Mrs. Wellington her own room. I swear my parents won't even notice, there are already so many of us in the apartment."

"You are such a sweet boy, Theo, and we appreciate the offer, especially Macaroni, as he longs to live near street vendors who drop bits of meat on the ground. But unfortunately we must decline. This is where Madame is most comfortable, and this is where we shall stay."

"But what will you do without having a school to run and students to care for?" Lulu asked.

"I'm planning to take up knitting, perhaps make Macaroni some sweaters for the winter; you know how much Madame loves an animal in clothes."

"That's it? You're just going to sit up here and knit dog sweaters?" Garrison asked in disbelief.

"I should think I'll also make the cats some sweaters

or scarves, and then a sweater for Madame, and finally a sweater or two for myself. After winter passes, I shall plant some vegetables, maybe try painting a portrait of Madame — in soft focus, of course."

"But what about Mrs. Wellington? What will she do all day?" Madeleine asked.

"At first I suppose she'll do nothing. She will remain a recluse in her room, but with time I expect she'll venture out, try on her crowns, and attempt to relive her glory days with a few extra afternoon nips."

"Will we at least be able to visit?" Theo asked hopefully.

"I should think not. I would prefer you to remember us as we've been, not as we'll be," Schmidty said forlornly. "But not to worry; should anything happen, the sheriff will keep you all informed."

"So this is it? The last supper?" Theo said.

"Maybe the four of us could at least meet once a summer," Madeleine suggested. "We could go to a nice dinner or a movie, or maybe even find a new school or camp to attend."

Hyacinth stared at her plate, awkwardly aware of

being left out of future plans. Of course, she really couldn't blame them, after what she had done.

"Yeah, I guess," Lulu said in response to Madeleine's suggestion. "But it won't be the same. It's weird, because I never even thought I liked this place, and now all I want to do is stay."

"I know," Garrison agreed. "I'm really going to miss all of it. Mrs. Wellington, Schmidty, Mac, the cats, the house, and you guys. No one else will ever get what we did here…no matter how much I explain it…and I kind of don't want to explain it, you know?"

"I completely know," Madeleine said with a smile. "And Garrison…"

"Yeah, Maddie?"

"Well," Madeleine said with cheeks as red as a beet, "since we're leaving tomorrow, since it's all ending, and we may not be in touch again, or at least not as often… I want to tell you…that I think you're…" Madeleine suddenly stopped. She couldn't quite bring herself to say what she wanted to, what she needed to. Instead she simply stared at Garrison, her heart aflutter and her palms sweating. In her mind she was screaming it, but her lips just wouldn't move.

"I think you're...too..." Garrison said with a wink.

Lulu, Theo, and Schmidty all smiled the kind of smiles that only friends can share. Hyacinth and Celery looked on curiously, with a mixture of shame, embarrassment, and unbridled envy. These were exactly the types of relationships, of friendships, Hyacinth had always tried to achieve. It was only as she looked at her classmates and the trust that existed among them that she realized they had all been right the night before. She really didn't know a thing about friendship. Not one single thing.

CHAPTER 25

EVERYONE'S AFRAID OF SOMETHING:

Automatonophobia is the fear

of wax statues.

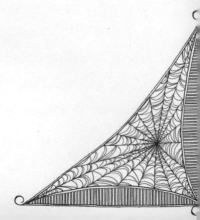

Madeleine, Lulu, Garrison, and Theo didn't sleep a wink. Sure, they all lay in bed silently, but none of them slept. They were far too busy absorbing every last ounce of Summerstone and School of Fear before it evaporated. They would never again see Mrs. Wellington, Schmidty, Macaroni, the cats, or the inside of this colossal and bizarre mansion. This was the end of an era, and an important one at that, and they didn't want to sleep away a single second of it.

Nearby, Hyacinth too lay awake. The little girl simply couldn't shake the sense of panic that was pulsing through her veins. She longed to sleep again on the floor of Madeleine and Lulu's room, but she knew that was not to be. Aside from the others being outrageously angry at her, the one thing they all had in common was about to disappear. This strange school she had only just started to know was to fade away, and Hyacinth for her part would return to her life in Kansas City with her family. But she would return with her same problem. And her poor brothers, sisters, and parents would suffer. Hyacinth couldn't bear the idea of her family not wanting to be with her but doing it out of obligation. No, Hyacinth thought, that isn't the kind of relationship she wanted to have anymore.

By breakfast time Theo, Madeleine, Lulu, and Garrison were bleary-eyed and gloomy, dreading the final goodbye that was fast approaching. As the foursome sat exhausted at the dining room table, Hyacinth slipped out the front door of Summerstone in an orange pantsuit. With Celery firmly seated on her left shoulder, the young girl forced herself across Summerstone's grounds. Twice she stopped and turned back. The idea of going down to the road alone made her vision blur with fear. But she knew it was the only hope of correcting what she had done.

Hyacinth began to whimper as the SVT rocked down the mountain. Time suddenly slowed to the speed of molasses as she felt her chest tighten. Drawing shallow and labored breaths, she stepped off the tram. Here she was, alone at the edge of a forest, just she and her ferret. Again Hyacinth turned and stepped back on the SVT. It was simply too hard. She couldn't do it. She stood on the tram for thirty seconds. What to do? There was a battle raging in her mind, and she didn't know who was going to win. Would her desire to change and right her wrong push past her wish to escape this overwhelming sense of panic? But would this feeling of panic, this force telling her to flee, actually stop if she returned to Summerstone? No, she would return as an outsider. Then she would go home as a burden. Hyacinth couldn't allow that to happen.

"Hello!" Hyacinth whispered at the edge of the forest. "Hello, Abernathy?"

Nothing.

"I'm just a girl with a ferret on her shoulder. Don't be afraid that you're a little bit older. Just 'cause you live

with the squirrels and the trees doesn't mean I think
that you have fleas. I'm not afraid that you may be weird.
I just need you so I can be cleared. So what do you say?
Will you join me today?" Hyacinth sang off-key.

While deciding what to try next, Hyacinth heard the
unmistakable sound of leaves crackling.

"I wish you wouldn't stop singing," Abernathy said in
the lightest, softest of voices from the edge of the forest.

"You like my singing?" Hyacinth asked with utter
shock.

"Oh, it's so lovely . . . like angels singing."

"You are the first person in my entire life to compliment my singing. Thank you."

"Thank *you*. Music is the one thing the forest lacks. I
listen to the birds tweet and the wind move, but it's not
the same as a voice carrying those beautiful melodies
into my mind."

"I wish I had my harmonica! I've never had such a
great audience before! You won't believe how much better
I am with a harmonica. Next year I'm asking for a guitar
for my birthday. I'm going to start a one-woman band."

"Oh, I do hope you come and serenade me."

"Yes! That would be so awesome! Maybe we could

even record it? Hyhy live from the forest!" Hyacinth said excitedly before she remembered the situation at hand. "Unfortunately, that won't be possible. We're all leaving. School of Fear is closing. Unless, of course, you agree to come back and give the school one more chance…"

"No," Abernathy said unemotionally. "I can't…I won't…"

"You know, we're not that different, you and I. You're afraid to be with people, and I'm afraid to be without them. But in the end I think it has more to do with us than with them. Do you know what I mean?"

Abernathy didn't say anything. He simply stared at the young girl.

"I promise, if you come back we can sing together every day. I may even let you into my band."

"Do you have a record player? Those Knapps promised me a record player if I'd help them, but they never came through. I knew I shouldn't trust people in matching sweaters."

"If you come to the school and give it a try, I'll do even better than a record player; I'll get you an iPod."

"A what?"

"You really have been in the forest *way* too long."

Much as the night before, Madeleine, Lulu, Theo, and Garrison did not touch their food. They merely pushed it around their plates while trying to take mental snapshots of every small detail of their time at Summerstone. One thing was certain: they would never again enter any residence of such peculiarity and originality.

"Excuse me," Hyacinth said loudly from the door to the Great Hall.

"Miss Hyacinth, I've prepared a plate for you and Celery," Schmidty said kindly.

"Would it be possible to prepare another plate?"

"Is Celery eating off her own plate now?" Schmidty asked suspiciously.

"No, someone else is joining us..."

"Oh, Hyacinth!" Madeleine burst out joyously. "I don't know how you convinced Mrs. Wellington to come down, but thank you. Saying goodbye to her will mean so much to us. Thank you again."

"Wow, that's pretty cool," Lulu agreed. "Kind of shocking, because I didn't think she liked you after you ruined her entire life and career, but thanks."

"Thanks, Hyacinth," Garrison said with an apprecia-tive nod.

"I don't forgive you, but I want to," Theo said sin-cerely. "And I've got to admit I will feel a lot better leav-ing if I can give Mrs. Wellington one of my famous bear hugs. So thank you."

"Actually, no one is leaving," Hyacinth said with a smile. "I promised him we would all stay here for the full summer term." And from behind Hyacinth came an ashen-faced man in filthy clothes.

"Abernathy," Schmidty mumbled in shock.

"He isn't ready for the full *Today* show experience, so no questions, guys," Hyacinth said, holding Abernathy's hand. "But he really loves music, especially my voice! We're even starting a band. We're still playing around with names, but we're thinking it best to keep it simple: A Girl, a Guy, and a Ferret. We've even started writing our first song. It's called 'Don't Be Jealous of My Ferret.'"

As Madeleine, Lulu, Theo, and Garrison smiled hopefully at Abernathy, Schmidty waddled over and set an extra place at the table.

"Welcome home, Abernathy. Welcome home."

Just in case Mrs Wellington
hasn't quite cured your phobia,
the story continues in . . .

SCHOOL OF FEAR
THE FINAL EXAM